PRAISE FOR *JUKES & TONKS*

"The world needs more jukes, more tonks, and more fine crime fiction—and this fast-paced playlist from Michael Bracken and Gary Phillips offers all of the above and then some. It's a #1 hit...with a bullet!"

—Josh Pachter, editor of *The Great Filling Station Holdup: Crime Fiction Inspired by the Songs of Jimmy Buffett*

"Whether it's Mississippi blues, Louisiana zydeco, or Texas country ballads, in *Jukes & Tonks* editors Michael Bracken and Gary Phillips have put together a diverse collection that swings, rocks, and rolls. These tales of revenge, murder, thievery, and double-crosses are set to a soundtrack dripping with nostalgia and atmosphere, where humid nights, dolled-up gals, and desperate men work their cons to a seductive backbeat. While twists abound and nothing is predictable, one thing is certain: *Jukes & Tonks* transports the reader to a world where the drinks are cheap, the dancing is close, and the music reigns supreme."

—Holly West, Anthony Award-nominated editor of *Murder-a-Go-Go's: Crime Fiction Inspired by the Music of The Go-Go's*

JUKES & TONKS

JUKES & TONKS

EDITED BY
MICHAEL BRACKEN
AND
GARY PHILLIPS

Down & Out Books
3959 Van Dyke Road, Suite 265
Lutz, FL 33558
DownAndOutBooks.com

The characters and events in this book are fictitious. Any similarity to real persons, living or dead, is coincidental and not intended by the author.

Cover design by Zach McCain

ISBN: 1-64396-184-5
ISBN-13: 978-1-64396-184-2

For Temple
My Love, My Muse, My Everything
—Michael Bracken

For Dr. English, who always knew the score
—Gary Phillips

TABLE OF CONTENTS

INTRODUCTION

It's funny when you write about music in prose. Reading a criticism of a John Lee Hooker record means you and your reader share an audio experience of what he sounds like; how his guttural growls originating in the Delta are like the moans of the ancient ghosts of slaves and hard times. His simple but direct lyrics weave themselves around those guitar licks he learned at his blues-baptized stepdad's knee. Otherwise you might as well be describing advanced trigonometry to a parakeet. But once that bird hears "Burning Hell" or "Never Get Out of These Blues Alive," its head will be bopping and clawed feet tapping.

If you've picked up this collection, perhaps you've experienced a juke or a honky-tonk or both. Maybe you've seen that kind of establishment on television or at the movies—that hilarious bit in the *48 Hrs.* flick where Eddie Murphy as Reggie Hammond walks into the western-themed redneck bar comes to mind. If you're a crime fiction fan, you might be curious to see what the wonderful and varied assortment of writers we've pulled together have accomplished between these covers. Because the one thing we know as crime fiction readers is the form is eminently adaptable, be it chicanery going down in the drawing room, on a neon-lit, rain-slick street or, in this case, what goes on once the band is through playing in that shotgun shack of a roadside joint, where a cold bottle of beer is rubbed against a sweating forehead for relief.

I'll not provide a blow-by-blow encapsulation of the stories in this anthology but will tell you, ain't a one of them disappoints. The writers here cover a lot of territory, even given the edict their contribution had to involve a tonk or a juke. The stories gathered here deftly evoke specific eras and thorny situations, laying down fully realized characters. There is syncopation of the word pictures they paint of various locales and the kind of folks who populate them that will keep you turning pages. These stories do what they're supposed to do—take you away and plop you down in worlds where the music not only enthralls from a compact stage, if there's a stage at all, but also provide the tempo to tales that are unsparing, heartbreaking, twisty and at times as dark as the night where the blinking sign offering live music is an invitation to the unexpected.

For it could be by the time your heels are crunching across the gravel as you walk up to the front door and the hot tunes are pouring forth, this might not exactly turn out to be the evening you had in mind. Well, at least it won't be boring. Come along now and drop right on in, sit yourself down, and thrill to this most assured collection, *Jukes & Tonks*.

—Gary Phillips
Somewhere in L.A.

AN ACHE SO DIVINE

S.A. Cosby

Hattie Mae saw the sun bouncing off the hood of the Plymouth Fury as it pulled into the gravel-covered parking lot of The Sweet Spot. The light spilled across the red surface like melting candle wax. Hattie Mae kept wiping down the bar between glances at her night-school workbook. This week there was a test for accounts receivable. She saw a slim brother climb out of the back seat of the Fury carrying a pair of drumsticks that he beat against the air to a rhythm known only to himself. A heavyset brother climbed out of the passenger seat. A handkerchief appeared in his hand like magic as he mopped at his brow and wiped his neck.

Hattie Mae moved to the end of the bar and gave the front window her full attention.

A tall, broad-shouldered brother climbed out of the driver's side of the Fury. His coal-black hair was conked and swept back from his forehead with a flourish. He wore a silver blazer like his bandmates but there was something in the way he carried himself that made his jacket seem to glow. A thin sheen of sweat covered his tawny skin. Hattie Mae thought it made him look like a movie star. Chester walked the way you expected a lead singer and guitarist to walk.

She watched as they grabbed their instruments from the Fury's cavernous trunk. They laughed, shimmied, and shook their way

3

up to the front door of The Sweet Spot.

"That bar ain't gonna wipe itself, Little Girl." Her daddy's voice boomed as he came out of the kitchen. Otis Jones nudged Hattie Mae as he walked by on his way to the front door.

"You turn your head any harder to peep out that window, it gonna pop off," Otis said.

Hattie Mae felt her cheeks get hot.

"The East Side Playboys!" Otis said as he opened the door. The trio lugged their equipment through the door.

"Shit, Otis, it's hotter in here than it is outside," Ellis said. He was the heavyset one.

Otis laughed. "It's hotter than this in Hell and I'll send you there if you keep running that mouth, son!"

Ellis chuckled and held out his hand. Otis shook it, pumping it up and down. Chester pulled out a cigarette and lit it with a gold Zippo.

"That fine-ass Sally still working here, Otis?" he said after taking a long drag.

"You mean Susie," Hattie Mae said. Chester took a drag off his smoke, then exhaled through his nostrils. Hattie Mae could feel his eyes on her through the smoke.

"She got married and moved out of Red Hill up to Richmond," Otis said.

Hattie Mae noticed how her daddy's shoulders stiffened.

"That's too bad. She had some pretty eyes. Make-a-man-think-about-settling-down kinda eyes," Chester said.

"Well, somebody did settle down with her. A good man," Otis said. He let the words hang in the air between them for longer than was comfortable.

"Uh...can we get some Cokes before we set up? We been driving for about four hours and my throat so dry I could spit dust," Fred said as he tapped his sticks together in a staccato rhythm.

Otis relaxed. "Sure. Hattie Mae, get Fred and the boys some sodas."

"With ice please," Fred said.

"Make mine with Jack, baby girl," Chester said. Hattie Mae glanced at him. He was looking at her but not the way she remembered him looking at Susie. Hattie Mae didn't respond but set about pouring their drinks.

By the time the band had finished setting up, the sun had set, and folks were trickling in like sand in an hourglass. Hattie Mae put away her workbook. She set about making sure the few booths and tables had napkins and ashtrays while Otis fired up the stove in the kitchen. The menu of The Sweet Spot was pretty simple because no one who stepped through the door had come there for the food. Fried chicken sandwiches on two pieces of bread and still on the bone. Pickled pigs' feet that sat in a big glass pickle jar at the end of the bar. Macaroni and cheese that Otis made with his mama's secret recipe.

Hattie Mae's mother had gone on to glory four years earlier, the day Hattie Mae turned seventeen. The cancer had eaten away at her in big monstrous bites. One day she was there with her big beautiful smile and sassy hips, then the next she was a wisp of flesh and bones in a bed that smelled like the sour mash her daddy used to make his corn liquor.

"Take care...of your daddy." Those were the last words Ardelia Jones ever spoke on this side of the veil.

Hattie Mae returned to the bar and leaned against the cash register. When she was little, she had been afraid of it. She'd gotten it into her head that it was going to bite off one of her fingers. Her daddy had choked on his drink when she'd told him.

"Girl, the only thing that cash register eat is money from fools that don't know when they done had enough," he'd said.

Couples started to pile into the place. The men walked across the pitted wood floor in cheap shoes shined to perfection. The women clicked and clacked their way toward the tables and booths in high heels they'd bought down at the Sears in the bargain bin down at the Sears. Tight Saturday night dresses that would lead to Sunday morning prayers of forgiveness. The Sweet Spot was the only place in Red Hill where black folks could go without worrying about ending the night with a white man's boot on their neck because they'd had the temerity to exist. A place where you could go at the end of the week and spend what you could spare to forget the world for a while. A world that never let you forget for one minute where you stood.

A few boys Hattie Mae's age came through the door, but Press Williams stopped one of them. Press was the bouncer, janitor, and assistant cook for The Sweet Spot. Hattie Mae hadn't noticed him come in but that was par for the course. For such a big man, Press moved like a ghost.

Otis had given him a job last summer when he'd gotten out of Coldwater Penitentiary. Hattie Mae knew the fact that he was her cousin and her mama's nephew was the only reason her daddy had deigned to hire the man. He walked around like he had a cord of wood on his shoulder instead of a chip. His dark skin rippled with rough-hewn muscle wrapped around his arms and chest like rigging rope.

"You ain't allowed back in yet, George. Otis say you got another week," Press said. His voice was deep and dark like the river that ran through the county.

"Aw, come on, Press, I said I was sorry," George whined.

"Ain't about being sorry. You need to learn how to handle you liquor. Another week oughta do it," Press said.

George didn't move.

"If I gotta get off this stool it's gonna be longer than a week," Press said.

George had balled up his fists, but he unfurled his fingers one by one.

"Come on, let's over to Mathews," George said.

"Shit, you can go. Me and Royal going inside. Them Playboys 'bout to make this place jump," Mack Chasen said. He gave Press his money and headed for the bar.

"Sorry, George," Royal Thomas said.

"Fuck this ol' rat hole," George said before stomping out the door.

Hattie Mae chuckled to herself.

"What you laughing at?" Mack asked. He was smirking at her with a light dancing in his brown eyes.

"Nothing. You gone let George sit outside all night?" Hattie Mae asked.

"He ain't come with us. Ain't my fault he got fighting, got his ass kicked, then threw up all over the dance floor. Fool was looking like a water fountain," Mack said before blowing air over his lips and imitating said water fountain.

Hattie Mae shook her head. "What you want, boy?" she asked.

"Let me get two tastes of your daddy's special brew and a dance later," Mack said.

"Drinks the only thing you getting, Mack. My daddy might wring your neck, he see you dancing with me," Hattie Mae said.

"Girl, you daddy love me. I always give him an extra half pound when I cut his meat at the store. He'd love to have me as a son-in-law," Mack said.

"How he gonna have you as a son-in-law when I ain't marrying you?" Hattie Mae asked.

"Ha, she got a point boy," Royal said.

Mack shrugged.

"My mama say a closed mouth don't get fed. That's all I'm saying about that. Think about that dance, girl," Mack said as Hattie Mae handed him two shot glasses filled to the brim with moonshine. He and Royal threw them back and headed over to one of the booths.

But not before Mack gave Hattie Mae a wink. Hattie Mae didn't have the heart to tell him he was wasting his winks. Her eyes were on somebody else.

"Good evening, ladies and gentlemen. We are The East Side Playboys, and we are so glad to be here at The Sweet Spot tonight! Now we just come up from Surry County and them folks down there know how to...." Chester paused before strumming his guitar.

"Twist and Shout!" He sang into the mic. The band launched into a bluesy rendition of the down-home classic. Bodies filled the modest dance floor as Otis turned the regular lights down and turned up the two lights with red cellophane over their clear shades. The magenta hue gave Chester a devilish appearance. Hattie Mae thought he was what ol' Lucifer would look like if he ever popped up behind her and tried to tempt her to throw away her virtue. Handsome and dangerous in equal measure.

The heat inside the building jumped from uncomfortable to unimaginable before the band was halfway through their first song. Press got up off the stool and opened the front door. He went to each of the casement windows and cranked them open. Her daddy went to the end of the bar and flicked a switch and two large green metal fans he had bolted to the ceiling came to life. They clattered and shook in time with Fred's frenetic movements on his sparse drum kit.

Chester had jumped down off the stage and was playing the guitar with his tongue. Right before he put the strings to his mouth, he'd locked eyes with Hattie Mae. She shivered. The crowd was moving in unison like some great amorphous beast. Dark faces soaked in sweat and split by wide smiles nodded in time with the beat.

"Looks like we gonna be able to eat for another week," Otis said as he nudged Hattie Mae with his elbow.

They were on their fourth song when the white girl showed up. She strode through the door with her chin up and her long black hair spilling down her back. Her eyes were hidden behind big frameless sunglasses that were less than useless inside the shadowy confines of The Sweet Spot. The music didn't screech to a halt like someone had bumped a record player, but Hattie Mae felt a change in the atmosphere. Hedonism was replaced by caution. Joy was replaced with suspicion. The men appraised her warily but with a hint of desire. The women glared at her like they had seen a cockroach in their ice cream. The girl didn't seem to notice. She took a seat at the table where Mack and Royal sat. Her white leather go-go boots were in sharp contrast to their Buster Browns. Mack leaned forward and whispered in her ear. Royal's face was screwed up in a knot.

Hattie Mae thought, not for the first time, how the road between the black side and white side of town was a one-way street. The girl wasn't the first white woman to find her way across Route 14 and she wouldn't be the last. White boys wandered in from time to time as well, drawn by the fantasy of the forbidden and made bold by the freedom their skin color afforded them. Mack came to the bar.

"Hey, let me get three chicken sandwiches and three shots."

"You sure you wanna be buying shots for Betty Anderson?" Hattie Mae asked.

Mack grinned like a jack-o'-lantern. "What, you jealous? You can still get that dance."

"Ain't nobody jealous of your skinny ass, Mack. But Jimmy Anderson ain't gonna let you get nowhere near all that Sears and Roebuck money," Hattie Mae said.

Mack threw his head back and howled.

"You laughing but the way I hear it he got more white sheets in his closet than he got on the shelves at the store," Hattie Mae said.

"Ain't nobody worrying about Big Jim," Mack said.

"You should be," Otis said. He'd popped up behind Hattie Mae like a phantom. Her daddy was almost as quiet as Press.

Mack stood up straight. "I ain't mean no harm, sir," he stammered. He grabbed his drinks and stiff-leg-walked back to the table.

Otis shook his head and clucked his tongue. "He don't need no part of that girl," Otis said. He wiped his wide hands on his apron.

"Huh," Hattie Mae said.

"What?" Otis asked.

"Nothing. Just, he said you liked him. I thought he was lying," Hattie Mae said.

"Just because he cuts me an extra half pound of meat don't mean we running buddies, but I don't want to see him hanging from a tree. Jim Anderson is about as mean a son of bitch you ever gonna meet, Little Girl. If it was up to me, I'd tell Miss Betty there to swing her hot hips on out the door," Otis said.

"Ain't her fault she's pretty," Hattie Mae said.

Otis snorted. "It's her fault what she do with it."

"I tell you what, the last time we was in Red Hill I don't think we had the right crowd cuz y'all know how to get it cracking. Now, if you don't mind, we gonna slow it down for a few. Here's a song we wrote, and we sure hope you like it," Chester said. He'd nearly sweated out his conk. His hair was laying across his forehead like a peacock's tail in repose.

He sat down his guitar and grabbed the mic. Ellis picked it up as Fred began a slow languid rhythm. Chester stepped off the stage again and put the mic to his lips.

To have a love so fine
Even if it's only from time to time
Oh, girl it's an ache so so divine

His voice soared to a falsetto on the last note of "divine." Ellis strummed the guitar, then abruptly stopped as Chester slid across the floor on his knees until he came to a stop in front of Betty Anderson. He sang the opening lyric again a cappella until the last note, where Ellis came back in with a vengeance.

Hattie Mae felt a fetid thing awaken in her chest. It opened its green eyes and spread its fibrous wings until they enveloped her heart. Of course, he'd focus on her. Not only was she the only snowflake in a sea of chocolate, but she was gorgeous. He was gorgeous. They were like magnets. It was natural for them to be drawn to each other. How could she be mad about that? That's just the way it was. Might as well be mad at a fish for swimming or a bird for flying.

Hattie Mae poked her head into the kitchen. "Daddy, I need a break."

"All right. Give me a minute to finish—"

She didn't wait for him to finish anything. She slipped from behind the bar and slid along the wall toward the exit. They didn't call it the front door because it was the only door. She tried not to pay attention to the couples pressed together, slow dancing to Chester's mournful baritone.

The air outside was so much cooler it made her skin pop up with gooseflesh. The moon hung in the sky like a sand dollar tossed in the air by John Henry in some forgotten tall tale. Hattie Mae bounced from one foot to the other as she smoothed her hair against her skull.

Don't be so damn dumb. What you getting mad for? Don't nobody own nobody, she thought. Cars zipped by like dragon-flies made of iron.

She clapped her hands together and went back inside.

Her breath caught in her throat.

The dance floor had emptied except for one couple.

Chester had one arm around Betty's narrow waist. The other hand still held the microphone. He was touching her. His free hand was just above the small of her back. Her hips moved in time with his. Her head swayed, making her hair undulate like endless waves against an imaginary shore. When the song ended, he did something that made Hattie Mae's stomach clench.

He kissed Betty Anderson right on her milky cheek.

The men hooted and hollered as Chester took a little bow. Many of the women clapped but the sound was hollow. Betty performed a little curtsy before stumbling toward the bathroom in the back of the building. Hattie Mae pushed her way through the crowd as the band launched into "The Blues Is Alright."

Betty was leaning over the sink. Hattie caught a sliver of her own reflection in the mirror above Betty's. Betty's face was bright red. An acrid scent wafted up from the sink.

"You're drunk. You can't handle that moonshine, can you?" Hattie Mae asked. Betty took off her sunglasses, ran the faucet, and splashed some water in her face.

"I'm okay," she slurred.

"Why are you here? Why'd you come here tonight?" Hattie Mae asked.

Betty pushed an errant lock of hair out of her face. "When I was in San Fran, I used to go to blues clubs all the time."

"Red Hill is not San Fran," Hattie Mae said.

"You telling me," Betty said.

"You sitting with Mack, you dancing with Chester. Are you trying to get them killed?" Hattie Mae said.

"What are you going on about?" Betty asked.

"You, here in my daddy's place sitting with colored boys when we both know your daddy is the grand wizard of what passes for the Klan around here," Hattie Mae said.

"Who's here gonna tell him?" Betty asked and Hattie Mae had to admit she had a point.

"Don't matter who tell him. It only matters if he finds out," Hattie Mae said.

"It's cool. You worry too much," Betty said.

"Why you dancing with Chester, anyway? Mack I can maybe understand, but not Chester. He ain't shit."

"I don't know, he's a hep cat. Kinda cute, ya know?" Betty said. Her voice had an upward lilt at the end of every sentence.

"Yeah, he real cute. He so cute last year he came through and got Susie Cunningham pregnant. She almost died having the baby. He ain't nothing but a low-down dog who thinks the world begins and ends at the tip of his dick." Hattie Mae spat the words out like they were soaked in arsenic.

"Hey, can you cool it? What's wrong with you?" Betty asked. Hattie Mae stepped closer to her. Betty turned to face her. Their noses were less than an inch apart.

"He ain't nothing. Man like that don't care about nothing. He ain't gonna care about you," Hattie Mae whispered.

She took a deep breath and inhaled Betty's scent. The shampoo in her hair. The soap she used. A special kind her daddy ordered for her through his Sears account. The Wrigley's she had just popped into her mouth. The heat from that mouth created tendrils that caressed her own lips. When Betty had come back home from San Francisco last January, she was not just different from the girl who had hung around her Daddy's leg while he tried to sell a washing machine. She was different from anybody who walked the dusty, dreary roads of Red Hill County.

They'd met in night school. Hattie Mae was taking bookkeeping; Betty was taking secretarial science. She swore it was only until she could persuade her daddy to smooth over the people at the college in San Francisco and make them readmit her. Even though the night school classes were segregated, Betty had stopped her in the hall. She'd seen Hattie Mae's copy of *On the Road* on top of her stack of books.

"Jack is such a bore. But Allen, if he liked girls, he'd be the bee's knees. He is so groovy," Betty had said.

"You...you met them?" Hattie Mae had asked. Betty had flashed those dimples at her as she nodded her head.

Soon they were making time to talk before and after class. She had talked to Betty about being torn between helping her daddy and finding her own road to travel. Betty had talked about wanting to get back to Haight-Ashbury. One night after class Betty had asked her if she wanted to go somewhere and hang.

"I know this place near where my grandparents used to live. We can hang for a bit. Talk some more. Do you smoke grass?"

Betty had asked.

"No, I don't mess with that kind of stuff," Hattie Mae had said.

"You mean not yet you don't," Betty had said with a sly grin.

"Hey, look, you're a really swell kid but ya know I'm all about living in the moment, man. Ya know, going with the flow," Betty said. The music from out front beat at the walls and thrummed up from the floor.

"What does that mean?" Hattie Mae asked even though she knew damn well what it meant. She felt her face get hot. Her eyes began to sting.

"I mean we had some fun, got our kicks. I'm all about free love but that's it, ya know?" Betty said. Hattie Mae thought if Betty said "ya know" one more time she might just scream.

"I thought you wanted to go back out west. I thought we were going to go together?" Hattie Mae asked.

Betty moved a lock of hair out of her face. "I never told you that."

"I know but I thought...I mean we..."

"We had fun, Hattie. We had fun," Betty said. The lock of hair fell in her face again. Hattie Mae reached out to move it, but Betty tossed her head back and the lock fell to the side.

Hattie Mae studied Betty's face. The flawless lines and the heart-shaped lips were still there, but it was as if a caul had been pulled from Hattie Mae's eyes, and she saw Betty for what she really was—a spoiled little rich white girl who didn't care about anything or anyone but herself, a selfish brat who could press Hattie Mae against the hood of her MGB convertible with kisses as hot as fresh asphalt one night and slow grind on Chester Harris the next. Betty had probably never even seen Jack Kerouac, let alone met him.

"You leaving with him? Gonna take him out there to the mulberry grove?" Hattie Mae whispered.

"He says he got some killer grass," Betty said as if that explained everything.

"He ain't the kind of guy to take 'no' for an answer." Hattie Mae grasped her left hand with her right. It was the only way she could keep herself from grabbing Betty and shaking her until she shook some sense into her. The things they had done to each other didn't fill her with shame. It was exactly the opposite. But she had known they couldn't be what they wanted to be if they stayed in Red Hill. California had been the dream but now she realized she had been the only one dreaming it.

"Who says I'm gonna say no?" Betty said. She smiled and stumbled back, hitting her butt on the sink. Hattie Mae felt tears fill her eyes. Betty touched her cheek.

"Hey, don't make this so heavy, okay?" she said.

Before Hattie Mae could respond, a woman barged into the bathroom. Betty and Hattie Mae moved away from each other as much as they could in the tiny room.

"I gotta pee!" the woman said as she tumbled through the door.

Betty deftly moved around the woman and out the door. Hattie Mae swallowed hard. Her throat felt like it was coated in glass.

"That white girl think her shit don't stink," the woman slurred from her seat on the toilet.

Hattie Mae got back to the floor just in time to see Mack take a swing at Chester. The taller man sidestepped the punch and reciprocated with one of his own. It caught Mack under his left eye. Press was off his stool and positioned between the two of them before Mack hit the floor. Royal grabbed his friend.

"Take him on out of here, Royal, or I'm gonna have to do it and trust me, he don't want that," Press said.

"Come on, Mack," Royal said. He half-carried, half-dragged his friend out the door. Mack and Hattie Mae exchanged a glance. They both saw regret in the eyes of the other but for different reasons.

As the night wound down and midnight became a fading memory, Otis turned on the overhead lights and the East Side Playboys finished their last song for a smattering of applause. Most of the folks had gone home or had migrated out to the parking lot. A few couples were still inside, cuddled up despite the heat.

Betty was still there too. She stayed as the band packed up their instruments. She stayed as Otis paid the Playboys and gave them a mason jar of his special blend for the road. She stayed as Fred and Ellis looped arms with the Marshall sisters.

"I'll meet y'all back up here in the morning," Chester said.

Betty crossed her legs as she sat all by her lonesome at a table behind him. Ellis peered over Chester's shoulder.

"Hey, be careful. This ain't Harlem," Ellis said. Chester gave him a grin.

"See you in the morning, Ace," Chester said.

Ellis nodded and went out the door with Fred and the Marshall sisters.

Chester turned to Betty. "You gonna be okay?" he said.

She stood and rolled her shoulders so that her hair fell down her back like a waterfall made of darkness.

"I'll be just fine," she said. She walked out the door with a strut and an extra twist.

"See ya next time, Otis," Chester said.

Otis didn't respond.

Hattie Mae heard Betty's MGB convertible roar to life. A few moments later the Plymouth Fury's engine joined the convertible's choir. Hattie Mae went to the door. She watched as they raced off into the night, their taillights winking at her like the eyes of demons sent to taunt her.

"I'm gonna help Press clear the parking lot. You start sweeping the floor, Little Girl," Otis said.

"I'm twenty-one," Hattie Mae murmured.

"What ya say there?" Otis asked.

"Nothing," Hattie Mae said.

Minutes later she heard her daddy telling the stragglers they didn't have to go home but they had to get the hell out of the parking lot. Hattie went in the back and grabbed the broom and the dustpan. She passed the phone on her way to the pantry. It hung on the wall away from the prying eyes of their customers. Most people in Red Hill had a party line. The Sweet Spot had its own private line. The novelty of it had proven irresistible, so her daddy had moved it from the bar to this dreary alcove.

Hattie Mae leaned the broom against the wall. Susie had told her how rough Chester had been.

"Girl, he barely gave me time to get my drawers off before he was all up in my guts," Susie had said. She'd arched her eyebrows when she'd said it, but the idea had sickened Hattie Mae. Betty didn't know what she was getting into. She had no idea what kinda man Chester was.

Before she could stop herself, before the gentle angels of her better nature could intervene, she grabbed the phone and dialed the sheriff's number.

A tired voice answered. "Red Hill Sheriff."

"There's a white girl, Betty Anderson, down on Cricket Hill Lane parked under them mulberry trees across from the old Carter place getting run through by a colored boy in a bright red Plymouth Fury. You might wanna get out there before Big Jim Anderson find himself with a half-breed grandchild," Hattie Mae said. She slammed the phone back in the cradle.

Hattie Mae went back out front and began to sweep the floor. She thought it was way past time for her to get out of Red Hill. Out of Virginia. Out of the past where the promises she had made to her mama held her tight and the memory of who her daddy thought she was held her down.

"An ache so divine," she sang to herself as the sounds of sirens screamed through the night.

EVERYBODY COMES TO LUCILLE'S
John M. Floyd

At exactly three-forty p.m. Tommy Garrison parked in the gravel lot of the roadside bar, climbed out of his car, and studied the ancient sign above the front door. LUCILLE'S, in tall red letters that had faded to an anemic pink. The building itself was a wood-frame, one-story structure without any windows, as plain and dreary as the almost-empty parking lot. It occurred to Tommy, and not for the first time, that nightspots everywhere looked sad in the daylight.

He pushed through the door, entered a dark tunnel of tables and stools, and—after his eyes adjusted to the gloom—took a seat near the middle of the wooden bar that ran the length of the room. Willie Nelson's voice crooned at him from the jukebox in the corner.

Tommy's childhood friend was the only other person there. She stood behind the other end of the bar, polishing shot glasses with a blue cloth.

"How was the vacation?" Tommy said.

Lucille McGee looked up at him, then went back to her task. "Too short."

"Sparky did a good job while you were gone."

"How would you know? You never come in here anymore."

"I was here last night."

She strolled over to face him, tilted her head, and studied him in the dim light. "What for? You ain't had a drink in five years." Then, smiling, "I remember you were partial to Jack Daniel's."

"And his whiskey, too." Tommy leaned forward on his stool and folded his hands on the bar. "As for last night, I was here to talk to Sparky."

"Why? You need a driver for a getaway car?"

He wondered if she was half-serious. "I'm done with all that, Lucy. I'm a hardworking citizen now."

"I heard you got fired again," she said.

"Actually, I quit."

"Sure." They locked eyes for a moment. Unlike her establishment, Lucille still looked good, Tommy thought. In a sassy, country kind of way. "What's the grin for?" she asked.

He shook his head. "Nothing. Thinking about old times."

"Better times." She glanced at the corner, where Willie was instructing mammas not to let their babies grow up to be cowboys. "Especially the old music."

"I thought that jukebox was for paying customers."

"I play it myself now and then. Remember, I get my quarters from the cash register."

"It's good to be da king," Tommy said.

Lucille put down the glass she was holding, snapped the dishtowel over one shoulder, and leaned back against a shelf below the bar-length mirror. "So what'd you talk to Sparky about?"

Tommy took a long breath. "Remember a guy named Clay Sherman?"

"You've mentioned him once or twice. I never met the man."

"That's because—no offense—I'm sure he thinks he's too big a shot for a place like this. But, lo and behold, he's been coming in here this week."

"News to me," she said. "I've been in Florida, warm and happy. Going back again next spring."

"With Dizzy?"

Her face hardened. "If Dizzy'd been there it wouldn't have been a vacation."

Tommy nodded. "Sorry," he said.

She made no reply. She was staring past him now, probably at something only she could see. Tommy didn't know all the details of Lucille's bitter relationship with her latest husband, but he recalled hearing that Dizzy McGee had wasted no time, once they were married, making her life miserable, and trying to take over her one financial asset: this tired little honky-tonk, halfway between two tired little towns in the middle of nowhere. Her name was still above the door and she still ran the place, but Dizzy told everyone he was the manager and decision-maker. Tommy felt for her but didn't know how to help, and she wouldn't have let him if he did.

"Where's Dizzy now?" he asked. "I saw both your cars in the lot."

She nodded toward the rear of the building. "In the office. Asleep, probably." She paused, still gazing into the distance, and added, in a low voice, "Dizzy's been acting strange lately. Even before I left on this trip."

"Strang*er*, you mean?"

"Yeah." No smile this time. "Er."

"Want to tell me about it?" Tommy asked.

"No." She turned and focused on him. "Who were we talking about? Clay Sherwood?"

"Sherman," Tommy said.

"Right. You said he's been here some this week."

He nodded. "The past three nights, around seven thirty. Sat right there on that once-fine-and-now-duct-taped barstool. At least that's what Sparky told me, late last night."

"Did he tell you why?"

"He said Sherman's trying to hire him."

For the first time Lucille's rusty armor cracked a bit. Her shoulders drooped. "Hire him to do what?"

"Didn't say. Legwork, probably. Sherman knows Sparky has

a lot of contacts."

She took the dishtowel off her shoulder and used it to scrub at something on the countertop. "I sure hope that doesn't happen. Sparky Rollins is my best worker."

"It won't happen. Clay Sherman made a pass at Sparky's daughter once, at a party. His married daughter. I doubt Sherman even remembers it."

"But Sparky does?"

"Oh, yeah."

The jukebox was between songs, and in the rare silence Tommy could hear the rumble of a truck going past, on the highway out front. Somehow it sounded far away. Part of a brighter, easier world.

"Is all this going somewhere, Tommy? I got things to tend to."

"All these invisible customers, you mean?"

"It's early—they'll be here soon."

She was right. Old and weathered or not, this was always a lively place after the sun went down. She was also right that it was time to state his case. He placed both hands flat on the bar. "I need to ask a favor."

"Come on, Tom. I got no money, you know that—"

"It's not money. I'm not broke, and I got a lead on a good job. An interview with the company's owner tomorrow morning. I even suggested he stop in here sometime."

"I'm sure your recommendations are keeping the place afloat. What is it you want?"

"Clay Sherman," Tommy said. "The reason I told you about him, long ago, is that he was running around with Yvonne. Still is."

Lucille snorted. "You should never have married that woman. What did I tell you?"

"You don't know Yvonne, Lucy. You never even met her."

"And I don't want to."

"Yeah, well, what you think of her isn't the point."

"What *is* the point? What exactly's going on, here?"

Tommy shifted position on his stool. "A plan," he said. "Like I told you, Sherman's been here the past three nights. Same time, same spot at the bar. Sparky told me he orders a shot of bourbon, talks awhile, and leaves. I expect him to be here tonight, too."

"Why? I'm back—Sparky won't be working tonight."

"Sherman doesn't know that."

Lucille pondered that for a moment. "What does he look like, this Clay Sherman?"

"He's kind of big, always in a suit or sport coat, dark hair, sour expression on his face. Looks down his nose at everybody."

"Except Yvonne?"

"Her too, probably. She just isn't smart enough to realize it."

From the far end of the room, an old wall-mounted clock chimed four times, louder even than the music. It sounded totally out of place in a backwoods beer joint, but Lucille had once told Tommy it had been her mother's, so there it hung. Tommy liked it. He liked things that had been around awhile.

When he turned back to Lucille, she had zoned out again, gazing absently at the front door. Tommy wondered if she'd ever considered taking her mama's clock off the wall, turning the *Open* sign to *Closed*, locking up, and changing careers. He would have, long ago.

"No more stalling," she said. "What is it you want me to do?"

He blinked, getting his thoughts back on track. "A simple request," he said. "When Sherman walks in tonight and sits down, I want you to smile at him, take his order..."

"Yeah?"

"And spike his drink."

Lucille blinked. "What?"

"You heard me."

"I can't do that."

"Why not?"

"Slipping someone a mickey is a crime," she said.

"This'll just be to make him nod off. No ill effects."

"Doesn't matter. It's assault."

Tommy rubbed his eyes, took another breath. "I really need this, Lucy. Nobody'll ever know. Ever."

A silence fell. Lucille was slowly shaking her head. Finally, she looked him in the eye and said, "Why?"

"Why what?"

"Why do you want him knocked out?"

"To discredit him."

"What does that mean?"

Tommy lowered his voice, even though they were alone. "Picture this. Sherman arrives, between seven and eight. You do some magic with his drink, he lays his head down on the bar and snoozes, and ten minutes later two of his top clients come in and see him in that state. They're straight arrows, these two, practically Sunday-School teachers."

"If they're so holy, what are they doing in my joint?"

He frowned. "You mean everybody doesn't come to Lucille's?"

"Why are they here, Tommy?"

"They'll be here because you'll call them, on the phone."

"And why would I call them?"

"I'm getting to that. You'll phone them, these two'll come in and help him, probably get him a taxi home or whatever, but then they'll fire him and tell everybody else what happened. Sherman's a financial counselor—people trust him to make smart decisions. Word'll spread—"

"And he'll be out of a job."

"That's right."

"So this is about revenge?"

Tommy shrugged. "It's about justice. And getting my wife back. If you knew Yvonne, you'd know she won't stick with anybody who doesn't have a steady income."

"What a princess. But you just told me you're out of a job yourself."

"No, you told me. I told you I'm interviewing with the head of a company tomorrow for a better one. And that's just a formality—he and I've met once already."

"So you said." Lucille studied him a moment. "What kind of company?"

"Does it matter? Come on, now *you're* stalling. Will you do this or not?"

She turned and gazed down the bar as if looking for spills, or stains, or maybe ghosts of a happier past. She folded both arms over her chest and blew out a lungful of air.

"I'll do it," she said. "I have some tranquilizers that'll work."

"How fast?"

"What would you need?"

"I don't know—a couple hours?"

She nodded. "I can do that."

"No after-effects?"

"Nothing to worry about. Maybe a headache."

"Okay, good. Great. Here's how I see it." Tommy paused to gather his thoughts. "Sherman comes in, orders his drink, and asks for Sparky. Probably in that order. You'll say Sparky's out, but he'll be back soon. Then you give Sherman a Mickey Finn, he dozes off, and a minute later you call this number"—Tommy handed her a slip of paper—"and tell the woman who answers that one of her business associates is in trouble and needs help."

"What woman?"

"Half the pair of clients I told you about. Her name's Miriam Gatewood, and the man who'll be with her is Bill Woodward. Just know that they're important clients of Sherman's and they'll be having a business dinner, the two of them, at the Glass Crown tonight until around eight. You'll ask them to come help their friend. They will, and when they see him, the damage is done. Mission accomplished."

Lucille mulled that over for several seconds. The Glass Crown was a restaurant in Addington, about six miles away in terms of distance and about a thousand miles away in terms of respectability. "How exactly do you know all this?"

"Sparky's not the only one who still has contacts," he said.

"Yeah, well, I have to make a living. If I phone these two people, they'll see my number. They'll know it was me and wonder how I knew to call 'em."

"No they won't." Tommy took an ugly cell phone from his pocket and set it on the countertop. "Use it once and get rid of it. It can get reception here, I already checked. Oh, and one more thing." He took out an old-fashioned three-by-five notecard. On it were printed the words *Stay away from Yvonne Garrison.* "Slip this into Sherman's shirt pocket, as soon as he passes out. I want him to find it when he wakes up."

"I don't like this, Tommy," she said. "This really could point back to me."

"How? Nobody but Sparky knows that you and I have a history together, and he'd never tell." Both of them knew this was true. Sherman didn't know her, Yvonne barely knew her, and Tommy had cut off most ties to Lucille McGee—Lucille Herring, back then—when he'd done time in the state pen. He'd stayed away to protect Lucille and her reputation. That, and not his conversion to teetotaling, was the real reason Tommy never came here anymore.

"I still don't like it," she said. "You know what they say about best-laid plans."

"This one'll work." He frowned. "Be sure to wash Sherman's glass, afterward."

"Really? I thought I'd bag it and take it down to the crime lab."

Suddenly, unexpectedly, both of them smiled.

"Why in the world do I still love you, Tom Garrison?" she asked.

At this, his smile turned sad.

"It's not because I deserve it," he said.

Tommy spent the next six hours doing what he did best: brooding about his wife and his life. At least he knew where she was, tonight. Yvonne played bridge every Friday night of the world, rain or shine, in sickness or in health. Which was fine with Tommy. When he got home from Lucille's he heated up some leftovers and watched a movie on TV until he nodded off in his recliner. He dreamed of his childhood and his high school days and of dating Lucille Herring all those years before they'd gone their separate ways, and of falling in with Big Nose Childers and the rest of that gang and stealing cars out of driveways and garages until they'd been caught. He could even hear the sirens again and see the frowns of the cops and the sadness in his mother's eyes the day he was sentenced to prison. And the confusion in his own eyes, looking back at him from the mirror, when he'd finally got out and gone back home.

In his dream he realized, maybe for the first time, that he shouldn't blame Yvonne for what she was doing. He was a bad husband and always had been and doubted he could change. Stopping the drinking and fooling around had been a small thing; what he needed to do was stop fooling himself. He wasn't even sure he still loved Yvonne anyway. All he wanted now was just to get back at Clay Sherman, to hurt him even worse than Sherman had hurt *him*.

When he woke up, he found himself wishing he hadn't met with Lucille at all. He looked at his watch. Ten forty-five. He could hear the shower running, upstairs. Apparently, Yvonne had come home while he dozed and was getting ready for bed.

Had Sherman come to Lucille's, as expected? Had the plan worked?

Tommy stood up, rubbed his face, and headed for the door. Time to find out.

He knew something was wrong as soon as he arrived. The outside lights were off, and Dizzy's Ford and Lucille's Toyota were still the only two cars in the lot. Eleven o'clock at this place was usually wild and rowdy and blaring hillbilly music.

Tommy parked and hurried to the front door. It was locked, a *Closed* sign hanging from its hook. But just underneath the sign was a yellow sticky-note bearing the handwritten words *Call Me.*

Tommy fumbled his cell phone from his pocket and punched in Lucille's number. A few seconds later her voice said, "Where are you?"

"Out front," he said.

"Hold on."

He heard footsteps from inside, and then the door opened. Lucille was standing there, an odd look on her face. She turned from the doorway and he followed her through the silent bar and into her office at the rear of the building. She dropped into the chair behind her cluttered desk, and he took a seat facing her. The only light was a crook-necked lamp on the desktop. Dizzy was nowhere in sight.

Tommy sat and looked at her, holding his breath. He was afraid to ask her what was going on.

As it turned out, he didn't have to. "It's been an interesting night," she said.

She had a glass of something in front of her on the desk, and she picked it up now and took a sip. She didn't offer him anything, which was just as well. He might've taken her up on it.

"Have you heard anything?" she asked him. "About tonight?"

He shook his head. His mouth felt dry. "What about it?"

"Fasten your seatbelt," she said.

"Okay..."

She drew a long breath, let it out, and put down her glass. "Your man came in a little earlier than you said—maybe seven— and sat down pretty much where you said he would. Big guy, black hair, nice suit, arrogant-looking. Never saw him before. He ordered a drink, kept glancing around. Before he could ask for Sparky and make me have to lie to him, I doctored his drink and he obligingly conked out, head on his napkin. I made the anonymous call to his clients at the Glass Crown, and they were

Good Samaritans just like you said. Came over right away."

Tommy was nodding, listening with rapt attention. He knew this wasn't going to end well—for God's sake, here they sat, the place closed down tight during peak business hours. But he held his tongue.

"Another thing," she said. "Just after he passed out and I called his two 'associates' at the restaurant, somebody on the way to the john accidentally bumped the edge of the guy's stool, just enough to move it a little, and a second later the guy toppled face first into the lap of the lady on the next stool—I don't know who she was. She yelped and whacked him on the head with the peanut bowl and he fell the rest of the way to the floor." Lucille paused. "Insult to injury, the offended lady stormed out and never paid me."

Tommy was gaping at her by now. "And that's where the people you called found him?"

"Yep. Lying right there on the floor."

"Go on," he said.

"Well..." She paused a moment. Her face had that strange look again. A mixture of shock and sadness and something else. Relief? He didn't know.

"While we were all standing around looking down at this poor bastard lying unconscious on my floor, the front door banged open and"—she fixed him with a stare—"it was like in the movies or something. Everybody just stopped talking, stopped doing whatever they were doing, and turned and looked. If music had been playing—I don't think it was, at that moment—I honestly believe it would've stopped too. The place went dead quiet."

"So who was it?" Tommy asked. "The cops?"

"I wish. It was a guy in a ski mask. He came through the door with a gun in his hand, walking straight toward us. 'Don't nobody move,' he shouted. And we didn't."

Lucille's face was blank. She was looking at the open door to her office, and Tommy could see her picturing the front door instead, and a masked thug marching in.

Tommy said nothing.

"After my heart started beating again," she said, "I pointed to the cash register and said, 'Take what you want. Just don't hurt anybody, okay?' He didn't answer me. He just looked past me, like he was searching for somebody, and then froze. I looked too, to see who he was staring at, and it was Dizzy. Dizzy was standing there, looking back at the guy. Their eyes held for what seemed like a long time, and then both of them..."

Tommy waited, and when she didn't continue, said, "Both of them what?"

"Both of them looked at me."

He stayed quiet then, not really understanding. Or maybe not wanting to.

"Are you saying Dizzy knew this man?" he asked. "Are you saying—"

Lucille's eyes had gone dreamy. In an unsteady voice she said, "Then the guy raised his gun and aimed it at me. And started walking again, walking straight toward me." She blinked and looked at Tommy. "He was going to shoot me, Tom. Kill me, right there in front of God and everybody."

Tommy realized he was holding his breath. "So what happened?" he whispered.

She cleared her throat. "You know how you used to always complain that it's too dark and loud in there? That you couldn't see anything in the dim light and couldn't hear anything over the music?"

"I remember."

"Well, apparently the guy with the gun couldn't see anything either. Maybe especially with that mask on, I don't know ..."

"Tell me what happened, Lucy!"

"He fell down," she said. "He tripped over the dude on the floor and fell flat. And on his way down, he hit his head on the edge of one of the tables. Knocked the hell out of him. Knocked him cold."

Tommy gulped. "So that was it? He didn't shoot anybody?"

"I didn't say that. He just didn't shoot who he intended to."

"What?"

"He shot Dizzy. Right in that fat neck of his. Killed him deader'n a fencepost."

Tommy gaped at her. "Are you serious?"

She nodded slowly. "When the guy landed on the floor, his gun went off, and I heard a moan and turned around and Diz was standing there spurting blood all over everything." She swallowed. "He died fast. So fast you wouldn't believe it."

The room had gone quiet. The two of them sat there and looked at each other.

"So you think Dizzy..."

"I think he hired this guy to come here and kill me. He looked at me to point me out."

"Why?"

"So the killer'd know for sure who to shoot."

"I mean why would he hire someone to do that? To get sole ownership of the bar?"

"I don't know. Dizzy was in with some bad people, up in the Delta. Maybe he thought I knew too much about all that. Or maybe he wanted my life insurance." She paused. "Hell, maybe he just wanted to get out of our marriage."

"If that was it, I guess he got his wish."

"I guess so," she said.

Tommy was still trying to process all this. "So...did you tell the police?"

"About my suspicions? Damn right I did. And when they took off the gunman's mask—like I said, he was knocked cold as a mackerel—I recognized him. Not his name, we don't know that yet, but I knew his face. He'd been here twice before, meeting with Diz. Once they came back here to the office, to talk alone."

Tommy didn't know what to say. As things turned out, Dizzy McGee was not only dizzy, he was evil. Not to mention unlucky.

"Bottom line is," she said, "if you hadn't come in here today with this stupid plan of yours, I'd be dead right now."

He realized she was right. Maybe she should've put a thank-you note in Clay Sherman's pocket, instead of Tommy's message.

Which triggered another thought. "What about Sherman? Did he ever wake up?"

"That part's a little crazy, too," she said.

"What do you mean?"

"Well, remember I said those people—Mr. Woodward and Ms. Gatewood—came and saw him lying there? Right after that was when the excitement started. And after all that, nobody thought much more about the drunk sleeping it off on the floor beside the unconscious killer. Someone called the police, and the next hour was a circus of cops and ambulances and reporters and questions. When things quieted down and everybody went their own way, Woodward and Gatewood picked up where they'd left off: they called a cab to come take the guy home."

"But—how'd they react to all this?"

Lucille shrugged. "I think they just felt lucky to still be alive."

"So...going back to my plan...you think they'll still be clients, after seeing their financial consultant passed out on the floor?"

"I think you're out of luck, there," she said.

"What do you mean?"

"The guy passed out on the floor wasn't Clay Sherman."

Tommy sat up straight in his chair. "What?"

"The two clients didn't recognize him. Said they'd never laid eyes on him before."

"But—if that's true—where was Sherman?"

"No idea. Not here, though."

He just sat there, blinking. "So somebody who looked like him—"

"Like your description of him," she said.

"—came in here instead? And got drugged?"

"Yep. How's that for bad luck? And not only that, he got whacked in the head by the gal sitting beside him, when he took his unconscious nosedive into her lap."

"Good God," Tommy said. "And we don't even know who he was."

"I didn't say that. I said I hadn't seen him before."

"So you do know who he was?"

"I know his name," she said. "That's a story in itself. After the police revived the gunman and hauled him to jail and the coroner carted Dizzy's body away and we were waiting for the taxi and your Sherman lookalike was still sprawled there like the dead body in a game of Clue, the female client—Gatewood—offered to pay his bar tab. I said no, forget it, you don't even know him, and it was just one drink, but she insisted, and the male client, who'd dug the guy's wallet out so they could give his home address to the cabbie, got the idea of paying me from the cash in the wallet. And since the guy's ID was right there in front of us, we looked at it. His name was Fitzgerald."

Tommy frowned. "What?"

"Morgan Fitzgerald. Works for a company called Harwood Transports." She shook her head. "Bet *he* won't come here again for a drink."

Having made that reasonable statement, Lucille fell silent, let out an exhausted sigh, picked up her empty glass, and wandered back out to the barroom.

Tommy sat there awhile longer, studying the paneled walls of the office. He found himself thinking about the people involved in this fiasco. Lucille, who would soon realize, if she hadn't already, that she was free as a bird for the first time in years; her sorry husband, who had somehow gotten exactly what he deserved; the clumsy hitman who had accidentally hit the wrong man; the sleazy but incredibly lucky Clay Sherman, who was probably out with his buddies someplace right now and drunk as a skunk; and Yvonne, who was likely at home thinking about Sherman. She sure wouldn't be thinking about Tommy. He also recalled, for some reason, the dream he'd had earlier tonight, about hearing police sirens in the distance, and realized that that part hadn't been a dream at all.

Mostly, though, Tommy found himself thinking about his scheduled meeting tomorrow with Morgan Fitzgerald. Morgan Fitzgerald, head of a local trucking company, who had apparently picked the worst of all nights to take Tommy up on his suggestion to visit a local honky-tonk named Lucille's. The fact that he looked a little like Sherman had never crossed Tommy's mind.

He could picture the expression on Fitzgerald's face when he woke up with an undeserved hangover and a knot on his head and found a note in his shirt pocket that said *Stay away from Yvonne Garrison.* So much for Tommy's future with Harwood Transports. As Lucille had said, plans—no matter how good they seem—don't always work out.

Tommy stood up, stretched, and followed her into the other room.

Lucille had poured herself another drink, he noticed, and was sitting on the barstool where he'd sat earlier in the day. He took the seat beside her.

"What a pair we are," he said. "The dumb husband and the grieving widow."

She shook her head. "You're not dumb, Tom. And I'm sure as hell not grieving."

Both of them smiled, sitting there together in the empty room. Tommy didn't think he'd ever been in here without music playing.

Without a word he put an arm around her, and she leaned her head against his shoulder. The sweet smell of her hair reminded him again of happier times.

"Sure you don't want a drink?" she said.

"I don't drink."

After a long moment, she turned to look up at him. "Want to go to Florida?"

Behind them, high on the wall, the old clock struck midnight.

JUNIOR'S JUKE

Penny Mickelbury

"Lord, I forgot how hot it gets down here!"

The clerk checking the young woman into Pascal's Hotel pulled her registration card toward him and almost choked. He quickly composed himself and said, "I hear it gets pretty hot in Chicago, too."

Charlene Hicks didn't miss much, and she didn't miss the desk clerk's reaction to the information on her card. "It sure does," she said, "but nothing like this. Then it gets so miserably cold that you forgot how miserably hot you were just a couple of months ago."

The clerk, whose name was William, smiled. "I can't cool it off that much, but we got real good air conditioning in the restaurant and in the lounge," he said.

"And that'll be just exactly cool enough," Charlene said.

"I hope you'll enjoy your stay with us, Miss Hicks," William said. He signaled the bellhop, gave him her room key, and before the elevator door closed on them, he was dialing the telephone. Then he had to check in three new arrivals, and by the time he got back to the phone Alex had hung up. William didn't blame him. Besides, he'd find out for himself soon enough.

Charlene turned off the still raggedy-as-shit main road onto the worse-than-ever, raggedy-as-shit road that led into the Negro community of Beatrice and stopped the car. Her hometown. Back after more than ten years away, and if it had changed, it wasn't for the better. The heat still shimmered up from the road, a mirage that could never blunt the reality. She drove on, knowing what she'd find when the raggedy road ended. No point in prolonging the inevitable. However, surprises sprang up on either side of the road, like the weeds that sprang up within the road: small but well-kept houses resided in the middle of well-kept fields. Nobody was getting rich in Beatrice, maybe not even prospering, but what Charlene was seeing was far from the disaster she'd expected. Then the road ended, as it always had, at the driveway into the parking lot of her father's juke joint. She slammed on the brakes.

"For once the lyin' SOB told the truth!" Charlene drove into the gravel and concrete lot toward the juke, now a large cinder-block square perched atop a concrete square. She hadn't believed him when he swore, *"I done made the place a palace! Wait till you see it! Come on back home, Charlene. Please!"*

She had the huge parking lot all to herself. She got out of the car and the moist heat almost knocked her back in. She slammed the car door, hustled to the front of the juke, and swung open the screen door. It was dark and almost cool inside. And it was empty. The jukebox was dark and silent. Homage to her three-days-dead father? She didn't think so. No matter what else was happening, there was always at least one drunk at the bar, one at a corner table, and music.

"How 'bout a cold drink on a hot day?" she heard from behind the bar.

"The coldest Red Rock Cola you got." Charlene smiled the reply and walked toward the bar.

"Why didn't you tell me you was comin', Charlene?"

"Didn't know I was until I was, Alex." She went behind the bar and hugged the old man. "How're you doing?"

"Still blind in one eye and not seein' so good out the other, but I'm still standin' upright." He gave her a pat on the back and the cold Red Rock, and she went to sit on a barstool.

"The place looks good. I thought he was lyin', the way he lied about everything." She looked all around, her memory seeing weathered and splitting pinewood walls, the hard-packed dirt floor, the tables, chairs, and bar stools retrieved from some junk heap. Now thick plywood covered the walls and ceiling, and the floor was smooth concrete. The bandstand actually was big enough to support a band and maybe an upright piano, and the room was large enough that everybody could dance. But where was everybody? "How come it's so empty, Alex? I know it's the middle of the day, but still—"

Alex opened his mouth to speak, closed it, and moved away. Charlene heard the screen door open and slam shut, heard heavy footsteps coming her way.

"I'm surprised to see an Atlanta Airport rental car in my parking lot, but very pleased to see such a pretty girl in my establishment!"

Charlene turned on her barstool to find fat, ugly George Flowers standing much too close. She leaned away, putting her back against the bar. "Did you say this was your establishment?"

He grinned, leered, and leaned in. "Yes, ma'am, I did, and yes, ma'am, it is. George Flowers, at your service." He leered another second, then turned and headed behind the bar. He walked to the far end, pressed a button and some kind of whiny music emanated from six big speakers that Charlene had failed to notice: one in each corner of the room and two wall-mounted behind the bandstand. With some real music playing...

"Can I pour you a Chardonnay or a Chablis?" George asked.

"You can pour me a bourbon up, with a side of ice water, Georgie Porgie." She grinned at him when he dropped the jug of rotgut wine. "Then you can tell me more about how this is your establishment."

"Ah...ah..." He stumbled and stammered and finally found words. "Alex! Get out here!"

Alex came from the kitchen, wiping his hands on his apron. "You need something, George?" he said testily.

"Did you know this...that she...who she was? Did you know she was coming?" George had started out sounding strong and irate, and finished whining.

Alex looked at him as if he were as stupid as he sounded. "She looks just exactly like she looked when she left here, so yeah, I knew who she was. And since her Daddy passed away three days ago, I guessed she might be coming."

"She don't look nothin' like she used to!"

"Yeah, she do. But then you was lookin' at her tits and her ass—beg your pardon, Charlene—so you most likely don't remember her face." Alex didn't try to hide his disgust and contempt.

"What are you doin' back there anyway?" George snapped.

"Filling up the soft drink cooler, and I could use some help."

"How did she know her Daddy passed away?"

"Say what?"

"I said—"

"Stop talking around me, talking about me like I'm not here!" Charlene stood up and faced George. "You have something to say to me?"

"No. Not really. I mean...I just didn't know you were coming, that's all. When you left you said you wasn't never coming back here!"

"And if Daddy hadn't died, I still wouldn't be back here. And you wouldn't be calling this 'your establishment,' would you?"

"Your old man gave me a lot of responsibility—"

"Did he give you this place?" Charlene asked the question quietly, gently even, and waited patiently the several seconds it took George to answer.

"We talked a lot about it. He was sick a long time—"

The screen door slamming open and bouncing off the wall interrupted him, and the hobbling walk-and-run gait coming toward her in the dimness told her who it was.

"Hey, Leroy," she said.

"Miss Charlene! You a sight for sore eyes, Girl!"

"I'm glad to see you, too."

"When I heard you was here—"

"Get outta here, Leroy!" George snarled. "I didn't call you to work."

"Hang on, Leroy," Charlene said. "I might need you." Then she turned to face George. "Alex said he could use some help stocking the cooler. And make sure you put plenty of beer in."

George looked at Leroy, but Charlene kept looking at him. "Me? You want me to stock the cold case?"

"You still work here, don't you?"

"Yeah. I guess. But...but I got an errand to run. I'll be back in—"

"You leave here now and I'll take that to mean you quit."

George sighed, shook his head, and stomped around the bar into the back, snarling that Alex had better hurry up and come help him.

"The jukebox still works, doesn't it?" Charlene asked.

Alex nodded. "George just unplugged it so he could play—"

"Then plug it back in and get the music going. I don't ever want to hear any more of that whiny shit in here."

"You got it," Alex said, then leaned in close and whispered, "George been stayin' at your Daddy's house last couple of days."

Charlene hurried over to Leroy and led him outside. She gave him the keys to her rental car. "Go over to Daddy's, Leroy, and nail all the windows and doors shut, please. You know where he keeps his tools, right."

Leroy nodded, then whispered, "Mr. George, he already done took some of Mr. Hicks's things. Got 'em in the trunk of his car."

"Then get 'em out, Leroy, and put 'em in the trunk of my car."

"Be my pleasure, Miss Charlene, and I'm surely glad you're back! It'll be just like old times in the juke tonight!" he crowed, and hop-walked away on the leg and foot ruined by polio.

"God, I hope not!"

I work for you like a Georgia mule,
My friends laugh and call me a fool,
Your kisses might be sweet as can be,
But before I let you make a fool outta me,
I'd rather drink muddy water, sleep out in a hollow log

Hot Mama Susie growled and hollered and whispered her way through a song—any song—especially "I'd Rather Drink Muddy Water." She wailed, "I'D RATHER DRINK MUDDY WATER!" She cried the words like they'd be her last. She let them rumble deep in her throat like they were some kind of beast wanting to break free. And she stood almost statue-still. Susie didn't move around much, and she almost never came down off the bandstand unless she was singing one of Bessie Smith's low-down, dirty songs. Then she took bets on how long it would take her to get some poor fool hard. But Muddy Waters was her song of choice the night Charlene's mama left Charlie Hicks and his juke joint for good.

It was a Saturday night in January, and everybody was thankful that the raggedy state of the building let in some of the chilly air. Everybody in the place was drunk, Susie and her bandmates included: Jimmie Lee Sanders blowing the jug and his twin brother, Jonnie Lee, on the fiddle. Charlene was worming her way through the packed crowd with the jug of moonshine as she had been since she was old enough to pour without spilling any on the floor. The cloth bag that held the money was slung across her shoulders. She didn't pour until she was paid, no matter who the customer was, and more than a few had tried to talk their way into a free pour. But Daddy's rule was that nobody got a free pour—not even the preacher—and he'd tried more than once. The dancers were wild, waving their arms all over, though one arm at a time as the other held tightly to the dance partner. Feet moved much faster, it seemed to Charlene, than the deep base beat set by Jimmie Lee's jug, and people tried to sing with Susie. Or out-sing her in some cases.

40

Every few minutes Charlene would glance toward the bar to see her mother, doing the pouring from back there, but the last few times, neither Mama nor Alex had been there, and Alex always filled in for Mama if she had to go relieve herself. Charlene made her way to the front door where Daddy reigned on a stool between the door and the jukebox, to tell him that Tubby Tillson was peeing in the corner, and a man she didn't know was carving initials into the wall behind the bandstand. Daddy wasn't interested.

"Where's your mama?"

Charlene shrugged. "Behind the bar, I guess."

"Don't be stupid, Charlene! If she was behind the bar, I'd see her, and I wouldn't have to ask you where she was!"

The bad feeling between Minnie and Charlie Hicks was worse than it ever had been, and they no longer tried to hide it. Not even Mama. And that scared Charlene. "Damn you, Charlie Hicks, you and your damn juke joint!" Minnie had screamed these words at a fever pitch some time during the early morning hours. And now she was gone.

Charlie sprung off the stool and plunged into the crowd, muscling his way through flailing arms, gyrating torsos, and jitterbugging legs, and daring anybody to spill "rotgut, cheap-ass moonshine" on him. His rotgut, cheap-ass moonshine. The crowd parted to watch Charlie bum-rush a guy straight out the front door, guiding him by the jacket collar and belt. The guy pinwheeled a few steps and bounced hard into a rusty red Chevy—cars were parked all the way up to the door, and whoever owned that Chevy would be the last one out this night, probably too drunk to notice the dent in the hood. The reason for the dent bounced up quickly, snarling and cursing.

"Gimme back my pistol, mother fucker!"

"I'll shove your pistol up your ass! You know you cain't come in here with no damn pistol, wavin' it all around like you in some damn cowboy movie!"

"He got a knife, too, Daddy," Charlene whispered. "He's the one I told you was carving in the wall behind the band-

stand."

Charlie pulled the pistol from his pants pocket, cocked and pointed it at its owner. "Gimme the knife, too."

"What knife?"

"The one you was usin' to carve up my back wall," Charlie said, and accepted the switchblade with more grace than it was offered. "Now go home."

"I cain't! The fella I rode here with is still in there with some woman, and I cain't walk all the way to Greer in the cold."

Charlie, knife in one pocket, pistol in the other, stroked his chin. "Naw, I guess you cain't." He stood aside, holding the door open. "Come on in, then, and get somethin' to drink. But behave yourself."

Nodding his thanks, the man stepped past Charlie and lost himself in the crowd that had forgotten all about him. "Go find your Mama," Charlie said to his daughter, for he had not forgotten that he hadn't seen his wife in too long.

Charlie went out the back door, promising patrons that she was on her way to refill the moonshine jug…and she would— after she found Mama. Or Alex. The stockroom, kitchen, and back porch were empty. Charlene stood outside in the cold, shivering, though more from fear than cold. Where were they, Mama and Alex? Then she saw a light flicker in the woodshed, and she ran toward it. And scared the shit out of Alex, who had just extinguished the kerosene lantern and was walking to the juke in the dark.

"What in hell are you doin' out here in the dark, Girl?"

"Lookin' for you and Mama! Where is she?"

"Go fill up that jug, Charlene, and get back on the floor."

"Where's my Mama, Alex?"

Alex sighed. "She's gone, Little Girl. Somebody was hurtin' her, and I stopped him, but she said she couldn't take no more and she said if I didn't take her to the bus station, she'd walk."

Charlene started to cry. "Was she hurt bad, Alex?"

Alex nodded. "Yeah. She was."

Then Charlene remembered some other things her mother

had said that morning: "Some nigger always got his hands on me, Charlie, and you don't give a damn long as you selling your moonshine." And how her father had replied: "Stop your complaining, Minnie! I'm tryin' to run a business!"

"And what about who hurt her? Did you hurt him back, Alex?"

"I just buried him behind the woodshed."

"Good! I'm glad!" Charlene hissed with all the anger her little ten-year-old body possessed. Then she broke into tears and howled.

Alex let her cry for a moment, then took her by the hand. "Now come on, let's get back to work. I'll tend the bar unless Charlie don't want me to."

The following day, Charlie Hicks beat Alex Worth so severely that he lost sight in one eye and suffered diminished vision in the other. Despite the beating Alex refused to say where he took Minnie, or where she was going. "But since she didn't have no money, Charlie, I gave her what little I had. And since she didn't have a coat, I gave her mine. And in case it matters to you, the bastard who raped and beat her last night is buried behind the woodshed. On your property."

The two men never again spoke of the night Minnie Hicks escaped. Charlie Hicks never discussed his wife's disappearance with his daughter, and Alex Worth kept his one, barely functioning eye on Charlene Hicks, who looked exactly like her mother, and who would make her escape from Charlie Hicks's juke joint one day, too. Unless she liked men pulling and grabbing on her all the time. Women didn't like that. Even women who went with men for money.

"I don't remember the last time we had this many people in here!" Behind the bar, Leroy was so excited that he was hopping to and fro on his good leg. The room was packed like Saturday night with a new band playing, instead of the middle of the day on Friday—the Friday of Charlie Hicks's funeral, which had been a succinct affair. The few who attended followed Charlene to the juke, but the bulk of the crowd now gathered there was comprised of those who had been waiting for the funeral to be over, people who attended church as often as Charlie Hicks had: just about never. So many people that Alex, Leroy, and George all were working the bar and barely able to keep up.

"Been a real long time!" Alex replied, taking stock of the crowd. "Some of these people I don't even know."

"I told you it was a good thing Miss Charlene came home!" Leroy said.

"If Alex don't know all these people, Charlene don't know 'em, either, and they don't know her," George snarled, "so stop talking 'bout how good it is she came back home. We were doing just fine without her."

"Sorry you're not happy to see me, George." Charlene had come in the back door and was pulling on an apron. "Where do you need me, Alex?"

"Why you ask him? Why you didn't ask me?"

"Take my place, Charlene," Alex said quickly, "so I can go check the cooler. We goin' through beer and soda like it was the Fourth of July."

"I wish we had food. We need a cook. We'd make a fortune today if—" Charlene started to say, but George cut her off.

"I had food! I tried to tell y'all, but you didn't want to hear it 'cause it was me sayin' it! But I had food—"

"You had some dime-store potato chips and pork skins that's prob'ly stale." Alex finally gave voice to the disgust he felt for George Flowers. "And you wanted to sell it!"

The crowd thinned, then grew again as people came and went. The band came at ten and played until two, and Charlene was glad to see the back of them. Way back when, Hot Mama Susie with a jug and a fiddle as back-up had sounded better than the piano, bass, and horn playing behind the singer whose name Charlene couldn't remember. And all day and night, people expressed condolences to Charlene. Some she remembered and some she didn't, but it didn't matter. She appreciated the gestures of kindness. She didn't get much of that in Chicago—from strangers or from people she knew. And the number of people who called her Junior! They had to know her whether or not she remembered them! As a girl, she'd hated being called Junior and demanded that people stop it! "I don't look like a boy so stop calling me Junior!" People didn't stop it. They just stopped saying it to her face. Then one day Alex told her she looked exactly like her mother and that's why people called her Junior. Charlene didn't know whether to believe him, but she liked the idea and stopped protesting.

George didn't hang around to help clean up after Leroy shut off the juke box and the last dancer and drinker had left. Alex asked where George had gone in such a hurry because he usually wanted to count the money. Charlene told him that she thought George had gone to her father's house, and for a moment Alex was too angry to speak. Then he erupted. "On top of all the other things he is, he's a thief, too! You can't let him—"

"He can't get in, Alex—I had Leroy nail the doors and windows shut, and he said he'll sleep on the porch to make sure he doesn't."

Alex gave Charlene a pat on the shoulder. "Leroy ain't no match for George."

Charlene gave Alex a pat on the shoulder. "He is when his bunk mate is a double-barrel shotgun. And if you sleep here and keep watch—"

"Then where you gon' sleep, Junior?" Alex exclaimed, realizing too late that he'd called her by the name she hated. He started to apologize but she waved the apology away.

"I have a hotel room in Atlanta, so I'll sleep just fine. Then I'm going to exchange my rental car for a truck and buy all the beer, Red Rock Cola, and every flavor of Nehi soda I can pack in. And that band that was here tonight?"

"You don't want 'em back tomorrow night," Alex said, not asked.

"I'd rather listen to the jukebox all night than them."

"I might could get Susie—"

"Hot Mama Susie? She's still around?"

Alex and Leroy nodded but added that Jimmie and Jonnie were long gone.

"If she can front that band from tonight, Alex—otherwise make sure the box is ready to rock. And what do you think about roasting, say twenty pounds of peanuts, and giving 'em away?"

"Make it forty pounds!" Alex and Leroy said in unison.

"That's a lot of peanuts," Charlene said.

"Eatin' peanuts makes people thirsty," Leroy said.

"Free peanuts make happy customers," Alex said.

"Then let the good times roll!" Charlene said, adding that real food, like fried chicken, needed to be on the menu. Soon.

There ain't nothin' I can do, nothin' I can say
That folks don't criticize me
But I'm gon' do what I want anyway
Don't care if they all despise me
If I should take a notion, to jump into the ocean
T'ain't nobody's bizness if I do

The crowd sang—shouted—the last line with Susie and she loved it. She sang the line again, repeated it, and let the crowd have the final word. She waved the band into silence. Since she'd already announced that this would be a Bessie Smith night, Charlene was unprepared for what Susie said when she stepped to the edge of the bandstand because she was remembering that Susie had been singing the last time she'd seen her mother... *I'd rather drink muddy water*... "I'm so happy to be playing for y'all tonight. It's like coming home, and I know I have Junior Hicks to thank. Your mama would be proud. You look just like her, you know," and Susie let the crowd whistle and cheer and foot-stomp for a while. "Junior's the one to thank for the peanuts, too! I got me a whole pile of 'em hid away to eat after the show." And she gave the crowd more time to show their appreciation, which was making Charlene more and more uncomfortable. She held up a hand to Susie to make her stop. Susie smiled, blew her a kiss, waved the band to get ready, and whispered into the mic, "I'm glad you still listen to your mama, Junior."

Charlene didn't remember the sound of her mother's voice, or anything she'd ever said, except to call Charlie stingy, mean, selfish, and greedy, and to tell him he had a small, narrow mind. And she didn't remember Susie ever smiling at her. She watched the woman work her magic on the crowd.

I need a little sugar in my bowl, I need a hot dog on my roll...
(And not no little one, either)
I can stand a whole lotta lovin', oh soooo baaaad!
I feel so funny, I feel so sad

Susie held out her hand for help getting down off the bandstand and the old-timers knew what was coming, and they were ready.

I need some steam heat on my floor
Maybe I can fix things up so they'll go
What's the matter papa, why you ain't hard
Come on and save your mama's soul
I need some sugar in my bowl

Nobody wanted to leave that night. They had to push people out the door, then out of the parking lot, reminding them to take the back way, not through town, with their lights out until they cleared the crossroads. There was no Civil Rights Movement in Beatrice, Georgia. They locked the front door, then sat at the bar, letting the fatigue drain away.

"This was a good night, almost too much for my eyes to see it all." She yawned then, so she didn't see the shocked look Alex gave her. She was operating on about three hours' sleep and was barely staying awake. "Can we clean up in the morning?" Charlene asked, "I'm about to fall on my face."

"We got your Daddy's place all cleaned up, so you don't have to drive to Atlanta," Alex said.

"What are you doin' here, Charlene? What do you want?" asked George.

"What I don't want, George, is you stealing from my father."

"You don't care anything about him!"

"I care even less about you, which is why I'm not letting you steal from him. Stealing makes you an ugly person."

Alex choked on his bourbon.

Even backed into a corner George remained confrontational. "You don't know anything about running a place like this, Charlene. At least let me help you run it."

"Right into the ground, which is where you were headed, with all your foolish talk about 'elevating the establishment and the clientele.' That silly-ass radio music and pork skins won't bring paying customers in the door."

"And you know what will?"

"You were here tonight, George. We had to push people out the door—"

"They were here paying respects to Charlie Hicks."

"Very few people liked my father, George, including you—"

"Why don't we finish this tomorrow, after everybody's got some rest—"

"I want to finish it tonight, Alex, so George can decide if he wants to come back tomorrow."

"You think you know so much," George snarled, "just 'cause you live up there in Chicago. You think you're better than us Atlanta folks—"

Charlene laughed a deep belly laugh. She poured herself a shot of bourbon and offered the bottle around. "Now you think you're Atlanta folks? We're seventy-two miles from Atlanta and it might as well be seventy-two-thousand miles. We're in Shithole,

Georgia. No stores where Colored live. Schools for Colored children four miles away and if their folks don't have a car, they have to walk, which many of 'em don't, so we got ourselves a bunch of uneducated Colored people. And the white folks keep a close watch on us like it was 1937 'stead of 1967, making sure we don't get too uppity. That's why I had to hide my pickup in the work shed, why we can't paint the outside of this place. No work but farming or cutting trees for the lumber mills, and no entertainment but this juke joint—"

"That's my point, Charlene, if you'd listen: people will come here no matter what we do—play the Atlanta radio station or have a fat old dyke sing."

"You got a lot of nerve calling somebody fat, George, and you don't know Susie Montgomery well enough to know who shares her bed. Do you even hear what comes outta your mouth?"

Alex gave her a hard look. What had been coming out of Junior's mouth all night was her Mama's words, exactly the way her Mama said 'em. "Uh, Junior, you feelin' all right? I know you're tired—"

"Hold your horses, Alex. George, do you want to work here or not?"

"Sounds like you plan on stayin'."

She hadn't planned on it until that very moment. "Yep."

"Why?"

"Because it's not Chicago. Because Charlie Hicks isn't here." Because I hate Chicago as much as I hated Charlie, she thought, thoughts she'd never shared with anyone. And because she missed the Juke, especially since she'd seen how it could be without Charlie, and these thoughts she *did* share.

"What are you thinking to do, Junior?" Alex asked.

The words and ideas poured from her: Fix up the kitchen and hire a cook, paint the plywood walls and the cement floor but leave the outside raw cinder blocks, lengthen the bar and hang a mirror behind it and string lights all around the mirror. Get a bigger jukebox with songs from the '40s, '50s and '60s.

Hang a sign over the door: JUNIOR'S JUKE.

"Is that all?" George mocked.

"We can afford these things, right Alex?"

Alex nodded, then said, "How long you been thinkin' this, Junior?"

"Just the last day or two."

Leroy looked all around. "How you see all that in just a couple a days?"

"I keep my mind open and all kinds of things come in. If you close your mind, nothing can get in," Charlene said.

"Junior...you know your Mama has left this world, don't you?"

"Daddy wrote and told me. That was a lotta years ago."

"You been sounding just like her all day, Junior! Like she was inside you. Her words are coming out of your mouth! Hold your horses! She used to say that all the time!" Alex was sounding a little frightened.

"I went to Chicago because that's where I thought she went, but she never made it. She never made it out of Atlanta. That beating she took—" She made eye contact with Alex and he nodded understanding. "I never saw her after that day. I don't even remember the sound of her voice." She yawned. "I'm going to bed. Well, George?"

He hesitated briefly. "I'll be here in the morning."

They all left through the back door together, George and Leroy heading toward the woodshed and through the woods toward their homes, Charlene and Alex walking through the woods behind the juke to Charlie's.

"Why didn't he ever serve food, Alex?"

"Because he didn't want to pay—to buy it or to have somebody cook and serve it. He said he had enough money and didn't need any more. And since he never spent any, I guess that was true." Alex stopped walking. "He left it all to you, Junior, and there's a *lot* of it. That's what George was looking for."

Charlene didn't speak, just resumed walking to Charlie's.

Where there was a light on. Where they heard singing.

"I didn't leave nothin' on in the house," Alex whispered.

They got to the house, stepped up on the porch, and the light went out. "Trouble in mind, I'm blue, but I won't be blue always. The sun's gonna shine in my back door someday," a voice sang. Minnie Hicks's voice melted into silence.

"Looks like everybody was waiting for Charlie to go," Alex said.

THE DANCE THAT DAMN NEAR KILLED JIMMY DELL BRAEBURN

William Dylan Powell

Part 1: Shotgun Start

Ronny Laughton knelt to tee up his ball, wincing as he stood. Then he squinted down the fairway as if trying to gauge the distance. In reality, he was trying to catch his breath. Bending down was tougher than it used to be.

"Need my rangefinder?" asked Uri Cohen.

Ronny waved him off. He'd been waving Cohen off all afternoon, but Cohen's private equity fund had somehow wormed its way into the deal by snatching up the company Ronny had wanted to buy first. So, like it or not, Laughton would have to deal with Cohen. Ronny didn't much like Cohen, who hailed from Boston and looked to Laughton about twelve years old.

Ronny gripped his club and lined up in front of the ball, taking a few practice swings.

He could feel the group's impatience. Uri Cohen. Ronny's CFO, Jenny Talbridge. Tim Rains, Ronny's unctuous lawyer. Bubba, the founder of the target company. Ronny knew they were all waiting on him to just hurry up and swing already. Just hurry up and let them finish the round and get home to their families. Just hurry up and buy Bubba's company and add it to the Texas Industrial family so Cohen could get his exit multiple and Bubba could retire and chase whitetails out in West Texas. They all stared at him, waiting. Wanting. Growing impatient.

But Ronny didn't give a shit. Taking his sweet time, he torqued his body around and unleashed a pounding drive that sounded like a gunshot.

"Jesus H. Christ at the rodeo," said Bubba. "I see how you spend your day."

"Nice poke, Ronny," said Tim Rains, teeing up his shot. They were silent as the lawyer hammered a long drive down the fairway, just shy of Ronny's.

"Listen, Bubba," said Ronny. "I have nothing but respect for what you've built, but we can't possibly go higher than seventy, what with your debt profile and the intense competition. Those refineries have less loyalty than a New Orleans whore. What am I really buying? Equipment and goodwill? Some trucks?"

Bubba kept silent, puffing on a cigar, but his face reddened.

They got into their carts and drove up to the ladies' tee so Jenny Talbridge could hit.

"Seriously," she said, teeing up. "We're talking seventy million here. I mean, it's none of my business how you live, Bubba, but I don't know many who'd turn that down. And I'm sure that leaves enough for you guys, Mr. Cohen." She swung the club, connecting hard and launching her ball into the distance.

Bubba got out of his cart, dropped his cigar on the cart path and mashed it out with the toe of his shoe. "Look, I'm clearly out of my depth here, and Mr. Cohen pretty much told me to keep my mouth shut today."

Cohen nodded. "Yep. Feel free to start any time."

"Sorry," said Bubba. "Y'all don't understand. My folks aren't just any refinery welders, they're turnaround specialists. Do you know what that means? When a plant goes down for two weeks to do maintenance, thousands of difficult projects gotta get done. Niche work that takes a craftsperson's touch, often high up on a tower and in the middle of the night; hot, cramped, and uncomfortable. Probably one in ten-thousand welders can do it. And it's not just the people, it's the culture. I know they look like wrench monkeys to y'all but, trust me, they're hard to come by, and plant bosses only want the best on the job."

"Thanks, Bubba," Cohen said, caking white cream onto his nose. "Look, Ronny, there's no need to insult us. This company is forty-two years old. We're talking serious brand equity. And, like Bubba says, serious talent. Talent that has, how'd you say it, Bubba? Serious stroke."

The group took off down the fairway, each in separate carts to make their approach shots. The breeze blew through Ronny's hair, the course verdant and well maintained. It was an expensive place where the PGA played once a year. He'd have been enjoying himself if he weren't so bored.

Ronnie knew his intellectual abilities were pretty much average—all save for one. In one area, he had always excelled: the ability to study almost any situation and, with enough research, find a hyper-efficient shortcut. As far as superpowers went, shortcut-finding wasn't super sexy. But he was good at it, priding himself on coming up with creative and streamlined solutions nobody else saw.

The group met back up at the green.

"Brand equity," huffed Ronny, lining up his shot. "Don't come at me with your marketing bullshit. I want to know what contracts your team has in place that I somehow missed making Deer Park Welding worth a penny more than seventy."

Bubba opened his mouth to respond, but Cohen cut him off.

"This is courtship," said Cohen. "Not hardship. Brand matters in downstream services. You reached out to us, remember? I have an offer in hand from Streeter, a strong offer, and we're meeting with Gulf Coast in a few weeks. You snooze, you lose."

"Stop talking, please," said Ronny. He tapped the ball gently, following through with his putt.

"Well done," said Tim.

"Look, Mr. Laughton, this isn't some anemic upstream service company hitting up operators with a begging bowl. Downstream is strong and you know it, so stop with the Persian bazaar antics. Seriously, this is going to go away for you and the price is only going up. I'm not negotiating. This is advice."

"Yeah, you finance types are known for giving the best free advice," said Ronny, shoving his putter into his bag.

Part 2: Enameled Lava Countertops

It was mid-afternoon when Ronny parked his Iridium Silver Mercedes S Class in front of his home on Memorial Drive. Yard workers wielding edgers, blowers, trimmers, and mowers had descended upon the place like a SWAT team, their faces covered like bank robbers' against the blazing sun and flying pollen. Grass trimmings and pollen hit Ronny as soon as he stepped out of the car. His nose began running immediately.

He lugged his clubs into the home's cavernous foyer, desperate for a tissue.

"We need to talking," said Amélie in her imperfect English with its thick French accent.

"Oh, hey, darlin'. Hang on, let me get settled."

"Yes, exactly. Zis is what we need to talk about. Ow I have settled, and now I am done with ze settling."

"Uh…Okay, baby. Seriously, just let me put my stuff down."

"Phew. You smell like a peeg."

As he walked back to his man cave to deposit his clubs, Ronny thought back on his first wife—a sweet Tennessee girl named Tanya Lynn. She'd have never talked to him that way. *Tanya Lynn would have had a cold drink and a smile waiting*, he thought. What she hadn't had, however, was tolerance for a brief indiscretion Ronny had had with a former office manager.

Ronny's sensible second wife, Alejandra, had been a different kettle of crawfish. With short cropped hair and two Ph.D.s, Alejandra had run the household like a Fortune 500 corporation. She also had summarily fired Ronny over lunch at the Rainbow Lodge, in the presence of three lawyers and two financial consultants. This after a Norwegian nanny had abruptly quit and written a detailed screed to Alejandra about Ronny's wandering eyes and hands. Ronny hadn't been able to stomach pan-roasted pheasant since that traumatic lunch ambush.

This left Amélie, whom Ronny had met on a boondoggle in Marseille.

Ronny set his clubs behind his office bar and blew his nose. Then he poured a double bourbon filled with chipped ice, wrapped a napkin around the glass and tied it in place with a rubber band. Taking a generous swallow, he started the long walk back up the hall where Amélie waited with her arms crossed.

Jesus, just look at her, Ronny thought. *I swear she's even prettier when she's angry. And she sure looks radiant this afternoon.*

Amélie wore a billowy white blouse and black slacks, and carried her usual afternoon glass of gin. Her forehead wrinkled as she crooked a finger at him and said: "*Regarde*," walking away.

Ronny followed, frantically considering recent peccadillos.

Amélie stopped in front of the kitchen and waved her hands as if revealing the prize at a gameshow. The diamonds on her tennis bracelet were blinding.

Ronny looked around the kitchen at the ziggurats of blue granite, brushed steel and high-end appliances that had, to Ronny's knowledge, never been turned on.

He raised his eyebrows in anticipation.

"Ze countertops you blind peeg!"

Ronny's eyes fell to the countertops, which looked to him like a gleaming, swirling hunk of blue and silver ice ten miles long with a small pile of magazines in the middle.

"You promise when we move in zhat we rip out zis trash and make ze new nice counters. Ow can I host properly with such garbage?"

Ronny thought back to when Amélie had moved in four years ago. He'd hired a Norwegian architect to walk the house with her in a carte blanche arrangement designed to take the sting out of moving her from the south of France to the west side of Houston. The granite had come from Serbia, if Ronny remembered correctly, and probably cost four times as much as the maid's car.

"Sugar," Ronny said, taking off his Callaway golf cap. He rested the hat on the countertop, then snatched it back up again, wiping off a small drop of sweat.

Amélie's scowl deepened.

"I don't know why you're so upset. We talked about it, but you never brought it up again. The house is your deal. You can do whatever you want to it." *Except move it to France*, he thought.

Amélie squinted in distrust, uncrossing her gym-toned arms and placing her hands on her hips. Her face was crimson with anger, and the sight of the little French woman in such a state of agitation made Ronny's throat dry.

"Honestly, sweetheart. We can get the ball rolling this week. I just want to see you happy." He toyed with his hat and studied the little red anger splotches on her neck and chest.

"Eet iz like I am a widow from ze war. All you do is work! You don't care to nozhing about me, ze house, none of eet! Why geev my heart to a ghosty man?"

Ronny's eyes fell to the magazines. He pointed. "Is this what you want?"

He picked up a catalog, written in French and printed on thick paper. His eyes being thirty years older than Amélie's, he couldn't read a word of it other than a large-print headline in English: "Enameled Lava Countertops."

Amélie drained her gin and walked to the wet bar. Ronny heard the tinkling of ice in a crystal glass as he flipped the pages. Every single one of the countertops looked alike.

He tossed the catalog back onto the counter. "Seriously,

babe, do whatever."

Amélie set her drink right on the counter, not bothering with a coaster. "I'm sorry for to screaming at you like ze crazy person. I just mees you very much. Rodeo. Golf. Shopping. *Le Texas est tellement ennuyeux!*"

Ronny started to say something, but Amélie cut him off.

"I already have estimate from Aksel," she said, pulling a thick sheaf of paper seemingly out of nowhere. "All you have to do is sign. Surely zis is not too much effort."

Ronny held the intimidating paperwork away from his face to read it. Mostly the complex estimate was in Norwegian, though a number of technical diagrams were included. The measurements were in metric, and of absolutely no use to a real American. After a few seconds of hunting and squinting, he saw a number at the bottom in U.S. dollars.

A number that clenched his stomach. A number that made the cost of the Serbian blue granite seem like a Billy Fucking Bookcase from Ikea. A number that a man with his many responsibilities, which included two ex-wives and various and sundry offspring, could hardly afford.

Still staring at the paper, he said, "Sugar darlin', that is ridiculous. No. No way. Nobody spends that much on countertops. Not Saudi princes. Not Elon Musk. Nobody. In all the planet, nobody has probably ever spent that much on goddamned kitchen surfacing. Because that would be fucking stupid. No fucking way."

He chucked the estimate and the catalogs down the hallway, where they scattered like leaves in a summer storm. Amélie was angrier than he'd ever seen her. Nostrils flaring. Tiny patches of sweat under each arm. A lock of her bangs dislodged from a clip, hanging in front of one eye. She picked up Ronny's bourbon and threw it down the hall where it broke across the concrete floor.

They embraced each other with the urgency and enthusiasm of boxers at the start of a match. The pair kissed passionately before disintegrating into a devastating Category 5 hurricane of negligee, golf tees, suntan lotion, gin, high heels, and passionate curse words right there beneath the blue Serbian granite. Which, the more Ronny thought of it, *was* getting a little tiresome to look at.

Part 3: Johnny Reb's

"I'm So Lonesome I Could Cry" by Hank Williams played overhead as Jimmy Dell Braeburn held down his usual stool on the far end of Johnny Reb's bar. He always sat right under a stuffed javelina that looked like it had been mounted by a first-time taxidermist; the skanky-looking pig wore a Lynyrd Skynyrd bandanna and sported a cheap cigarillo jutting from its yellow-toothed maw. Jimmy Dell had named the javelina, with typical Jimmy Dell creativity, Lynyrd.

When neither Cody, Knox, nor Jasper were off shift, and Emilio the bartender got sick of listening to Jimmy Dell's braggadocious bullshit and busied himself at the far end of the bar, Jimmy Dell held long and meaningful one-way conversations with Lynyrd the Stuffed Javelina about women, the meaning of life, the superiority of Dodge trucks, women, Glock versus 1911 pistols, which Chuck Norris movie was the best (even Lynyrd agreed it was *Lone Wolf McQuade*), and women.

Johnny Reb's was a small, low-slung concrete building near the Houston Ship Channel, surrounded by an endless landscape of belching, blinking refineries and petrochemical plants. The place always seemed open, except for Sunday mornings, and had hardly changed over the years even as the rest of the Houston area had plunged headlong into the future. The sign out front read: "Johnny Reb's: Where you wind up when things go South."

Other than the small stage, which lit up whenever a band played, the only light sources inside the windowless bar were several neon beer signs, a small lamp by the cash register, an old jukebox—within which the newest song was by Alan Jackson—

and the light above one wonky pool table. The tiny dance floor was almost too dark to dance on.

The entire wall opposite the bar featured a not-quite-professional mural of Willie Nelson, Waylon Jennings, George Jones, and Johnny Cash—each figure cartoonishly recognizable but not quite right. Much like your dance partners, the visages got easier on the eyes as the night wore on. Which, many patrons postulated, was why the dance floor was kept so dark.

"Jaybird!" yelled Jimmy Dell.

Jasper Sirmon squinted as he stepped out of the sunlight and into the little honky-tonk. He took off his Amoco cap and bought two mugs of Guadalupe Gold from Emilio, who was busy polishing glasses at the front of the bar. Then Jasper made his way back to Jimmy Dell.

"You ready for Baton Rouge?" Jasper said, sliding one of the beers over to Jimmy Dell.

Jimmy Dell downed the beer he'd been drinking, which had been nearly full, then brought the Guadalupe Gold closer. He hiccupped. "Shit. Them Louisiana boys won't know what hit 'em. I'm 'a weld them crawfish-eaters out of their raggedy old boots, steal their shifts and their sisters, triple my per diem on a Booray game, get some OPP wearing my PPE and look that weld-inspector in the eye like I wish a motherfucker would."

"Humble as usual," said Jasper, throwing a pair of dirty gloves onto the bar.

"Humble? Shit, I'm the best god-damned turnaround welder in Texas."

"For the love of Christ," said Jasper, looking up at Lynyrd the Stuffed Javelina and hoping he'd somehow come to life and make Jimmy Dell shut up for five goddamn minutes.

"I remember this one old job in Corpus Christi. Huge turnaround. Red hats up our ass. The project manager..."

Jasper waved his hands. "Whoa there, hoss. Before you get going on one of your war stories, Bubba wants...are you listening?"

"Aw," said Jimmy Dell. "Ain't that sweet? Look at them two, will ya?"

"I Believe in Love" by Don Williams had begun, and a hunched-over, gray-haired couple began slow-dancing beside the bar. Their hair shone pink and blue and purple in the reflection of the neon signs, the man carefully balancing between his long-time bride and an oversized aluminum cane.

Jasper snapped his fingers. "Hey, look at me. Yes, it's adorable, pretty sure it's this bar that aged 'em like that. They're probably in their thirties. Listen, Bubba wanted me to tell you, since apparently you don't even answer text messages from the owner, that you need to be at the gate for headcount in Lake Charles at three a.m. sharp tomorrow. And that's everyone. Fat Pete. The Rabineaux twins. That crew from West Texas. Gear and clear heads and ready to go, and no bullshit. And we'd better shine, old son. Rumor is them Gulf Coast boys are gunnin' to run us out. We need this business every year to make our numbers, so, seriously, three a.m. sharp at the gate, ready to roll. Ten-Four?"

Jimmy Dell set his beer down and looked Jasper square in the eye. "Motherfucker, who you talkin' to?" He stood, grabbed Jasper by the collar and marched him out the door.

The parking lot looked like a used-truck dealership, with each vehicle backed into its respective parking space as per standard refinery protocol. The theory is that by parking backward, a refinery worker could escape more safely, and quickly, if something blows up and you need to get away fast. Which only rarely happened at a refinery but happened just about every night at Johnny Reb's.

The pair reached Jimmy Dell's custom Dodge Power Wagon, its license plate reading WELDBOSS. With a beep, the lights blinked, and Jimmy Dell opened the back seat.

"Don't you know I'm the best damn flame man this side of the Mississippi?" The back seat was packed solid with suitcases, coolers, a case of Dr Pepper, three pairs of boots and several sets of coveralls. "This eagle's ready to fly, old son."

Jimmy Dell shut the door just as a red Mustang convertible pulled into Johnny Reb's caliche parking lot. The car kicked up a cloud of dust as it parked on the back side of the building by the dumpster. The dust cleared to show two middle-aged women who looked like they'd just stepped out of a Pinto Ranch catalog—pastel ropers, silver and turquoise jewelry, and a complete lack of shits to give about Jimmy Dell and Jasper. One had long blond hair and the other had skin like *cafe au lait*.

The blonde talked on the phone as she threw open the door to Johnny Reb's, the other flicked a cigarette butt into the parking lot as the pair made their way inside and let the door slam behind them.

Jasper turned to Jimmy Dell. "I'm serious. Three a.m. at the front gate in Lake Charles."

Four hours later, Jasper squinted at his phone. "Shit, I gotta roll. And you do too," he said, poking Jimmy Dell in the chest.

Johnny Lee's "Lookin' for Love" serenaded a tiny table littered with beer mugs, wine glasses and empty tequila shots. The girls had introduced themselves as Marci and Darci, which sounded unlikely to Jasper but as a happily married man of thirty years he didn't really have a dog in the hunt. Jimmy Dell, however, had dug into a stool between them like a WWI infantryman in the trenches.

"You leaving already?" said Jimmy Dell. "The band's about to come on!"

"I am leaving," said Jasper. "And you are too."

"I most certainly am not, good sir."

Jasper leaned closer. "You know that last possible moment in the evening when you can still go home, and everything turns out fine the next day? This is that moment. Cash in your chips, Kemosabe."

"Well excuse me but fuck you, you're not the boss of me."

Darci stood, shaking out her hair. "Pardon us, boys. We're

63

going to freshen up." The two made their way through the cigarette smoke toward the ladies' room, holding hands.

"Technically," said Jasper, "I am the boss of you. And if you weren't so damn good at your job, I'd take you out in the parking lot and whoop you like a rented mule."

Jimmy Dell smiled, eyes glassy from the tequila. "Son, I wish you would. Skinny motherfucker I'd put that goofy smile through the goddamned wall." He slammed his mug on the table, sloshing beer onto Jasper's boots.

Emelio had sensed the situation going south in a way only a bartender can. Throwing a dish towel over his shoulder, he stepped from behind the bar and made his way to them.

"Y'all good or what?" he asked.

Emelio was a former boilermaker who'd done three years in Huntsville for aggravated assault. He had "HATE" tattooed on the knuckles of one hand and "HATE" also tattooed on the knuckles of the other. Just in case anyone got the mistaken impression he was a complicated man.

"We're good," said Jasper, shaking his head. "I was just leaving. Some of us work for a goddamn living." Jasper laid three twenties on the table and left.

Later that evening, Marci, Darci and Jimmy Dell all three slow-danced to Amy Grant's "Could I Have This Dance" together. Which was weird with three people, all eyes in the tiny bar locked onto the trio. But this arrangement was necessary because, at this point, Jimmy Dell could hardly walk. He had his head buried in Marci's intoxicating tangle of frizzy hair, as Darci held him from behind and rested her hot cheek against the back of his neck. The three swayed back and forth as Marci ran her long, red fingernails down Jimmy Dell's cheek. At one point, as their circular dance route brought them near the back of the bar, Jimmy Dell gave Lynyrd the Stuffed Javelina a thumbs-up, not that anyone else knew what he was doing.

The trio's reverie was disturbed by a cacophonous thumping and crashing of drums and cymbals erupting from the stage. "Check, check…" a man with a mullet said into a microphone. The stage lit up like a full moon.

"Howdy folks," said the man with the mic. The amps were so loud it was like the voice of god, clearing Jimmy Dell's sinuses and causing him to shake some of the cobwebs out of his brain. He kissed Marci on the forehead and stumbled back to his seat.

"Y'all ready to burn this motherfucker down?" said the man.

Jimmy Dell let out a yell that said he was.

A man at the bar yelled: "Fuck you, *punto!*" and threw a beer bottle, which shattered against a back wall behind the stage.

"Thank you very much," said the singer, casually brushing glass from his mullet. The band adjusted straps, tweaked settings, sipped drinks, and got into the zone.

Possum Patrol wasn't a full-time band. The lead singer was a maintenance superintendent; the lead guitarist a pipefitter and so forth. But they did decent Southern rock covers and could hold their own in a fistfight.

When they launched into Marshall Tucker Band's "Can't You See," Darci leaned in close and kissed Jimmy Dell's neck, eventually working her tongue into his ear as Marci screamed above the music: "Hey, y'all wanna go someplace quieter?"

In the parking lot, it was one of those hot, humid Houston nights where stepping outside was like getting licked by a dog. Marci and Darci pulled Jimmy Dell toward the Mustang, caliche crunching beneath their feet. The car, shiny and red earlier, was now dusty and bathed in the pallid yellow of a rickety security light. Flares from surrounding refineries flickered like fireflies.

"Well, now, ladies," he said. "I'm afraid this is where I leave ya."

One of the girls, he wasn't sure which, put a hand on his crotch. This didn't change his mind, but it did shut him up. At the car, leaning against the trunk, the two kissed him at once, Jimmy Dell lost in a blissful, roiling ocean of lips, tongues, softness, and perfume. But after a few minutes, he pulled his hand from Marci's shirt and looked at his watch. It took a few seconds to read the blurry readout: seven after ten.

He gently pushed Marci back and said: "Seriously, y'all. My boss is an asshole, but he's right. Time for this old boy to drag up. Not that y'all aren't lovely as a couple of little old bluebirds."

The warm Gulf breeze was still drying their saliva on his neck as both women squirmed from his arms and trotted away, their footsteps crunching hurriedly in the dirty parking lot. The lot spun slowly as Jimmy Dell searched for them, hearing nothing but the sound of crickets in the weeds and the muted thumping of the band inside. Eventually, he saw Marci and Darci several feet away directly beneath the light. Marci lit a cigarette as the two leaned against the building.

"Oh, come on now," Jimmy Dell said, squinting to see them. "Don't pout, little darlins!"

He took a step forward, holding his arms out. "I'll be back by Halloween. We can all dress up…"

That's when three more figures appeared beneath the light. Figures much taller, and wider, than the ladies. Jimmy Dell shook his head to make sure he wasn't seeing things. Then one of the figures stepped forward and swung a two-by four as Jimmy Dell's vision went black.

"What the fuck took you guys so long?" asked Darci. None of the men replied, busy with their work.

The sound of the two-by-fours hitting Jimmy Dell Braeburn reminded Darci of the way her mother used to beat rugs when she was cleaning the house back in Texarkana.

Marci turned to Darci and asked, "You got any gum?"

A few days later Amélie answered the door to find a blonde, about her age, in a sweatshirt and tennis shoes. She drove a dirty red car, and Amélie was not amused to see she'd parked in the driveway—a presumptuous act which Amélie expressly forbade contractors from doing at all times.

"Hello," said the woman. "Is Mr. Laughton available? Tim Rains, the lawyer, sent me. I was told to pick up a package."

Amélie opened the door and gestured the woman inside, not bothering to respond. The click of her high-heeled shoes on the polished concrete had the sound of a metronome as she marched the woman through the foyer to the kitchen.

"Oh, wow, I love y'all's countertops," said the blonde.

"Ronald!" Amélie screamed toward the stairway. "Delivery!" And with that she disappeared into the bowels of the home, leaving Marci unattended.

Ronny thumped down the stairs with a thick Manila envelope. Dressed in casual slacks and a sport coat, he handed the envelope to the woman, who ripped it open and dumped the contents on the blue granite countertops.

"Really?" asked Ronny. "You're going to count it here?"

"Shhhh," she said, mouthing numbers silently. As she leaned over the counter to concentrate, Ronny glimpsed a tattoo where the woman's sweatshirt rode up a few inches. *What is that?* he wondered. *A snake? No, a dragon? A snake eating a mouse that was wearing a sailor's hat?*

"Do you have a card?" he asked.

Stuffing the cash back into the envelope, Marci rolled her eyes. "Nope," she said. "Sure don't." And with that she walked out.

Negative Equity

Ronny sat in front of Uri Cohen at Ouisie's Table. Ronny ordered the shrimp and grits with sweet tea and Uri a Southern-style egg sandwich. Uri closed his eyes. "Go ahead, you fucking bull shark. Let's get it over with."

"What?" asked Ronny.

"The gloating. We both know it's coming, so let's have it."

Ronny just shook his head. "Industrial work is a fickle

business. I'll take good luck where I can find it."

Uri waited a moment for Ronny to say something else. When he didn't, he shrugged and took out a stack of papers. "Eleven contracts out the window," Uri said, shaking his head and arranging papers on the table. "It's unprecedented in this industry to my knowledge. A perfect fucking storm."

"Where's Bubba?" asked Ronny.

"Pouting at his deer lease in San Angelo." Uri took a bite of his sandwich, then wiped his mouth. "The guy's a wreck."

"Yeah, I can see how getting a check for forty million could really ruin a man's day," said Ronny.

"Don't be a dick. We both know this is a fire sale. I oughta take it off the table just on principle."

"Don't threaten me with a good time," said Ronnie. "Word on the street is without this guy Braeburn, a lot of the greybeards didn't want to work there anymore. The crew pulled off the turnaround project just fine, but right afterward a bunch of experienced hands jumped ship. Said it just wasn't the same. I'll have to put lipstick all over it."

"Whatever," said Uri. "If I'd have known one little-tobacco chewing shmuck was such an asset, I'd have put him in a golden fucking cage. I mean, the guy must have been the best goddamn welder in Texas! Gets beat up in a bar fight and POOF! Tens of millions in contracts gone. Apparently the poor fucker sees double now."

Uri leaned closer, assumed a serious expression and pointed at Ronny. "Where were you on the night in question?"

Ronny shrugged, his attention focused on his grits.

Uri chuckled. "I'm kidding. For real, though, you're getting a deal. Streeter walked. Gulf Coast is glowing like an expectant mother with a bunch of new talent. I have never seen a single line worker impact a company's valuation so much. It just doesn't happen."

Ronny swallowed and wiped his mouth. "Amazing."

Uri set his sandwich aside and went from paper to paper,

scrawling signatures with his Mont Blanc pen and shaking his head. "You couldn't have gotten a better deal more quickly if you'd planned this with a team of NASA scientists."

Ronny's phone lit up. The name on the screen read AKSEL TRYGSTAD. "Pardon me, I have to take this," said Ronny. "It's my countertop guy. One thing I've learned over the years, kid, is that nothing beautiful comes cheap."

RETURN TO SENDER
Gar Anthony Haywood

The St. Louis County Sheriff's deputy who'd come out to take the report was the one named Thorn, and Thorn was dubious, because who the hell wouldn't be? But he never gave Binny any trouble or made him feel foolish for calling it in. He was a total professional.

"Can you describe the stolen item, Mr. Binny?"

"Describe it? Come on, deputy, I just told you: it was a fucking jukebox. You know what a jukebox is, right?"

"Yessir, I do. Approximate size and weight?"

Lewis Binny was trying to contain himself. Some lowlife assholes had broken into his eponymously named bar off U.S. 2 in Stoney Brook Township, Minnesota, and, along with several thousand dollars' worth of booze, had stolen his late father's jukebox, the one that had been sitting near the door off the parking lot, next to the candy machine, since the fall of 1961. It had been a birthday gift to the old man from Binny's mother Grace. Binny was angry enough now to chew nails.

"I'm going to take a guess, okay? About five feet tall, three feet across and three feet deep. Weight, two hundred and change. A lot of change. They would have needed a refrigerator dolly to get it out of here."

"They?"

"Well, assuming the Hulk only exists in comic books..."

71

Then Deputy Thorn nodded, Binny's point taken.

More questions followed. Jukebox manufacturer and model number (Seeburg HF100R-D), approximate value twenty-five hundred dollars, without records, three grand with), thieves' point of entry (the back door, through the storage room), etcetera, etcetera. Binny answered every inquiry, keeping his head but making plans to castrate somebody as soon as an arrest was made. *Binny's* wasn't much, in point of fact, it was a dump that barely kept him in corn flakes and cigarettes, but it was all Binny had to remember his parents by, and the jukebox was a huge part of the joint's musty, wood-paneled charm. Shaped like a cheap prop in a bad science-fiction movie, all curved plexiglass and chrome, the Seeburg was no fucking Wurlitzer, but you could drop a quarter in it every night and have it spill three singles of your choice in high fidelity stereo, rain or shine. As long as "D6" wasn't one of your selections, anyway, because that button combination had stopped working eight years ago. Binny had never bothered to find out why.

Most of the kids who came into the bar were wholly unimpressed, of course. There was no Taylor Swift 45 to load into the machine and who the hell under the age of fifty had ever heard of Bobby Vinton? But it wasn't the kids who were keeping the place alive, in any case—it was their parents and grandparents, and they fed the box nightly to stir the ghosts of Ray Charles or Johnny Cash as they drank up Binny's beer and ate his mediocre food, sometimes even moved to dance across the sawdust floor with whomever would accept the invite. So there was more to *Binny's* than the juke, but not a lot more. It was going to be missed, and no one was going to miss it more than Binny himself.

"I'm sorry, I didn't hear that." Binny's mind had wandered, eyes fixed on the dusty patch of checkered linoleum where the Seeburg had been sitting only nine hours before.

"I asked if you have any idea who might have done this," Thorn repeated.

It was a good question with no easy answer. Binny knew a

lot of local Neanderthals brazen enough to break into his bar for the booze, but none stupid enough to take his father's jukebox on their way out the door. Because why? What the fuck was a thief going to do with a seventy-five-year-old jukebox filled with records by people long dead?

One name did come to Binny's mind, though.

"Beats the hell out of me," he told the deputy.

They dropped Binny's jukebox getting it off the truck. One of the two planks they were using as a ramp split right down the middle, and before Cyril or Nelson could catch it, the machine toppled sideways to the ground like a tranquilized elephant. Cyril thought Peoria would be furious, but she didn't seem to care.

"That's too bad," was all she said.

Cyril figured the juke had to be worth a couple grand, at least, in working condition, but it wasn't Binny's money Peoria had been after. It was blood. She'd sent Cyril and his baby brother out to rob her ex-husband's joint just to hurt him. They'd been divorced for more than eight years but Peoria was still getting over the job Binny's lawyer had done on her, using one lousy, five-month affair with a clerk at the local lumber yard to deny her any right to alimony. She got a four-figure lump sum and a 2002 Chevy Cruze out of the deal and that was it. The lump sum vanished in less than a year, the Cruze went belly up eighteen months after that, and Peoria had had her panties in a bunch ever since.

Opportunities for her to stick it to Binny were few and far between but she took every advantage whenever one presented itself. Important pieces of her ex-husband's mail that got mistakenly delivered to Peoria served as kindling in her fireplace; joint credit card accounts that should have been closed long ago stayed open just long enough to make a dumpster fire of Binny's credit rating. As Peoria's latest beau, Cyril had heard about it all, ad nauseam, fair warning that if things didn't work out between them, he ran the risk of being similarly abused.

But he was willing to take the chance. Peoria was a vindictive bitch, all right, but she filled a pair of jeans and a low-cut, sleeveless blouse like nobody's business, and she could ride Cyril's raging wild stallion as long as he needed her to stay in the saddle. In other words, she was special, and a man had to make certain accommodations for special ladies, like committing crimes that served more to injure the victim than enrich the perpetrator.

There was no way to make Nelson understand, however. Cyril's little brother looked upon Peoria as just another greedy, backstabbing whore with a killer bod, and robbing *Binny's* just to get a dozen cases of liquor and an ancient music box full of old records made no sense to him.

"This is stupid," he kept saying, from the moment they'd broken the lock off the bar's back door to when they started the truck's engine up to make their getaway. "This is just damn stupid!"

And now that it was all over and they were in the clear, everything having gone exactly as planned with the exception of dropping the goddamn jukebox off the truck while unloading it, Nelson's attitude hadn't changed one bit. Here he was in their mother's garage, he and Cyril drinking Binny's beer while admiring the brightly lit façade of Binny's broken-down Seeburg jukebox, complaining as loud as ever.

"Stupidest thing we've ever done."

"Jesus, man, are you ever gonna stop?"

"No. Why should I? You say let's do a job, I say let's go. We're brothers, we're a team. Always have been, always will be. But this? Putting our asses on the line for what? Five, six grand, tops? Just to fuck up some poor guy we barely know?"

"We *know* Binny. He's an asshole."

And that much was true. *Binny's* was a regular stop for them both; they'd been drinking there since before Binny and Peoria had even divorced, and the barkeep was no friend to either of them. In fact, Binny seemed to treat them like trailer trash, like

74

that sorry highway rest-stop of his was intended for a higher class of people.

"Yeah, he's an asshole," Nelson agreed, slamming back another swallow of Binny's Fulton 300. "But so what? I ain't never given a damn about Binny and neither have you. Only reason you care about him now is 'cause Peoria's still got a hard-on for him."

Cyril put a finger up, not wanting this conversation to go off the rails. "I think you'd better hold up right there, Little Brother."

"It's the truth, Cyril. She used us."

"Okay, so she used us. What of it? Six grand is still six grand, ain't it?"

"Except that it *ain't* six grand! It's four thousand dollars' worth of beer and whisky and a broken-down music box we could maybe get fifteen hundred for on eBay, if we're lucky."

"Fifteen hundred? That thing's vintage!" Cyril said, waving a hand at the Seeburg. "It's a one-of-a-kind collector's item."

"It's a piece of shit. It was a piece of shit before we dropped it off the truck and it's an even bigger one now." Nelson got up from his chair and dropped another quarter in the machine, his third of the night. Just as it had the first two times, the jukebox responded to his choice of three songs with a grinding wail, forty seconds of music from his last selection, and then silence.

"We could fix it," Cyril said.

"No. We couldn't."

"No, not *us*. I mean, maybe we could find somebody to fix it. Then we could sell it."

Nelson just shook his head, looking at Cyril like he'd lost what little of his mind he had left. "Stupid."

Handy White thought he had seen the Seeburg before. He didn't do much work on jukeboxes—slot machines and typewriters and old school arcade games were more his speed—but he was the only freelance repairman within a hundred-mile radius of

Minneapolis/St. Paul who would touch the things, so he saw his share.

"Looks like somebody dropped this out of an airplane," he said.

The guy who'd called him out to this storage facility way up in Stoney Brook—a short, beefy white man with a ratty gray beard and lopsided gut—just shrugged.

"Never ask a woman to help you move something heavier than a breadbox."

Handy nodded and smiled, as if he didn't know bullshit when he heard it. "You had this thing long?"

"About ten years."

"How did you find me?" He kept his eyes on his work as he posed his questions to lend an air of innocence to his curiosity.

"Google, man, what else? Four-star rating on Yelp. Next closest repairman was in Rochester and he wanted seventy-five dollars just for a quote. Did I make a mistake?"

"No, no. Just wondered, that's all."

The damn thing *had* been dropped out of an airplane. The lower half of one side panel was crumpled and crushed, and loose shards of the juke's broken glass fascia were floating around its insides like kidney stones. The main load mechanism was off its rails, several records were badly scratched and one—having been jarred completely from its slot—was cracked nearly in half. And these were just the things Handy was able to determine in his first five minutes of poking around.

All the while, as he pressed on with his assessment, the Seeburg's owner, "Jay"—if that was his real name—watched him like a hawk, peering over his shoulder into the guts of the machine as if he might, at any moment, have some expertise to impart. Either that, or he feared Handy would clean out the coin drawer and flee the storage unit with seventeen dollars and twenty-five cents in cold, hard cash.

When Handy eventually buttoned the Seeburg back up and gave him his written quote, the white man's jaw dropped just as expected, but then he did something else that took Handy completely by surprise.

"All right," he said. "How soon can you do it?"

"Seven hundred and eighty dollars? You gotta be shittin' me," Nelson said.

"It's an investment," Cyril said.

"Investment my ass. How do you figure that?"

"One, because we're gonna end up with something we can sell for three times that much. And two, we ain't gonna pay no two-bit nigger repairman seven hundred and eighty dollars to do shit."

"We're not?"

"Hell, no. I gave him a two-hundred dollar deposit and he's gonna have to be happy with that. If he's not, he can talk to our lawyer." Cyril laughed.

"After the work is done," Nelson said.

"After," Cyril agreed.

"How long did he say he was gonna have it?"

"Three weeks, maybe less. He's gotta order parts."

"Good. Should give us just enough time to find a buyer."

"Actually, I think I've already found one," Cyril said.

"Yeah? Who?" Nelson saw the grin on his big brother's face and started laughing. "Aw, hell."

Eight days after the robbery, Binny looked up to see Peoria sitting at her favorite booth, waiting for him to come around to take her order. He hadn't seen her come in and was in no fucking mood. Business was in the toilet, the Sheriff's Department was no closer to finding his father's jukebox than they were the remains of Jimmy Hoffa, and the last thing he needed was his ex-wife dropping in just to twist the knife. And he had no doubt that was the purpose of her visit, because the only time she ever came around anymore was to watch him squirm beneath the weight of her gaze and the foulness of her breath.

"Kinda slow in her tonight, ain't it, Bin?" She already had a Marlboro lit and she blew the smoke up and off to the right with exaggerated flair. She thought moves like that made her sexy, just like the streak of green in her auburn hair and the plunging neckline of the patterned blouse she was wearing, but it all just made her cheap and mildly amusing.

"And it just got a lot slower. What do you want, Peoria?"

"I want a drink and some time to relax. Is that a crime?"

"No, but murder is. And if you don't drink your drink and get the fuck out of here in fifteen minutes, I'm gonna strangle you."

She laughed as he walked away and was still laughing when he came back with her glass, a Vodka cranberry with crushed ice. Some things never changed.

"Thank you." She took a sip. "I heard what happened and I feel just awful. I had to come by just to see for myself if it was true." She turned her eyes to the other side of the room, where the discolored patch of linoleum flooring marked the old Seeburg's former resting place like a gravestone. "And it is, ain't it?"

"Yeah. It's true." By now, anyone who made *Binny's* a regular stop had spread the word about the robbery, and the most conspicuous part of its take, so it figured Peoria would have heard about the jukebox being gone. Still, Binny had to wonder, just as he had when Deputy Thorn of the St. Louis County Sheriff's Department had first planted the thought in his head: *You have any idea who might have done this?*

"It's a wacky world, ain't it?" Peoria asked, taking another draw from her glass. "I mean, who would think to steal a *jukebox?* Heavy as those things are? It just takes all kinds, don't it?"

"Eight dollars, Peoria."

"But I guess you could always buy another one, couldn't you. It wouldn't be the same one, not like the one your daddy gave you, exactly, but similar."

"You know, you could save yourself a lot of grief by just telling me where it is now," Binny said, done with his ex's fun and games.

"I what? I don't—"

"I'm just saying. If you know who's got my juke, the time to speak up is now. Because if anything bad happens to it before I get it back, and I find out you had something to do with it, I'm gonna put every power tool in my garage to work making you regret it. You understand?"

"You're crazy!" Peoria finished her drink, crushed her cigarette out in an ashtray like a bug. But she was shaking as she did it. "Why would I want to steal your old piece of shit jukebox?" She started to squirrel her way out of the booth but Binny blocked her exit.

"Eight dollars," he said, holding out his palm.

Handy had a full plate of work to do. A 1960s-era Philco entertainment center, an NCR cash register, a coin-operated motorcycle kiddie ride—but he kept going back to the Seeburg.

"I don't get it," Quincy Hardaway said, watching Handy work. "If you're thinkin' the man can't be trusted, why you doin' the job for him anyway?"

It was a question Handy would have asked himself, had their situations been reversed.

"I'm not really doing this for him. I'm doing it for the machine. For me and the machine, both. Does that make any sense?"

"No. That don't make any damn sense at all."

Quincy raised his mammoth body up from his chair and sauntered back over to his side of the shop. When Handy started waxing poetic about "machines," he often lost his audience, and Quincy was no exception.

The two black men shared a storefront building that Quincy owned outright in the Frogtown area of St. Paul, and each ran their own business on one half of the floorspace. *'Ploitation Station,* Quincy's video and memorabilia shop devoted to the cinema of the 1970s blaxploitation era, resided on the east side and Handy's antique repair business was conducted on the west. Twenty years his junior at forty-four, Quincy was Handy's best friend, and he never had a problem letting Handy know when he was acting a fool.

And what else could you call investing twelve days of labor and hundreds of dollars in parts on a service job for which you did not expect to get paid in full?

Handy didn't understand it himself. He just knew the Seeburg needed him. Sometimes, he took a job more for the owner than the old, mechanical object requiring repair, and sometimes it was for both. But every now and then, the only reason he said yes was the object alone. He didn't feel pity for it, exactly, but an obligation to correct a wrong, to undo whatever damage time, or neglect, or malice had done to it. If the work was challenging, that was all the better, but it wasn't about the work. It was about the outcome. It was about justice.

The Seeburg needed justice.

Tomorrow, Handy would be finished with his repairs. He would have to call the owner and return the machine to the Stoney Brook storage locker from which he'd taken it. Until then, he would run the jukebox through its paces, playing one 45 record in its 1960s-era honky-tonk collection after another— the Righteous Brothers, Roger Miller, Roy Orbison—and try to think of a way to avoid being played for an even bigger fool than he already was.

Binny had Peoria spooked.

"We've gotta give it back. He knows it was me!"

"Oh, we're gonna give it back, all right," Cyril said. "Soon as we see three thousand dollars in cash."

He didn't know why he hadn't thought of it sooner. Holding

Binny's beloved jukebox for ransom would be a lot less work and a lot more profitable than trying to unload it on the open market. It would be a win-win for everybody. Binny would get his juke back and Cyril and Nelson would get three grand to split between them. Instant gratification, no eBay or craigslist hassle necessary.

"He'll never do it," Peoria said. "He's not gonna pay you to get somethin' back that already belongs to him."

"*Belonged* to him," Nelson said from across the room. He had another bottle of Binny's beer in his hand and the History Channel on the TV. "The juke belongs to us now."

"It don't matter. He won't pay."

"We'll see," Cyril said, taking a swig of Jack on ice, also courtesy of Binny. "That boy Handy called me an hour ago. He says our girl's good to go."

Early the next evening, Handy returned the Seeburg to the same storage facility from which he'd picked it up. He knew there'd be no electrical outlet in the unit so he'd brought a gas-powered generator with him.

"What the hell's that for?" the juke's owner asked, annoyed. There was a younger man with him he'd introduced as his brother "Vince" and together they painted a very unsettling picture.

"I thought you'd want to see it work. Or were you just going to take my word for it?"

There was nothing the guy who called himself "Jay" could say to that, so he simply nodded his head. Handy plugged the jukebox in and cranked up the generator. From all appearances, the three men were the only ones in the facility at this time of night and the generator's drone was like a dash of black ink against a white page of silence.

Handy told the two white men everything he'd done to the Seeburg to return it to working order, dropping a quarter in the slot as he spoke. He punched six selector buttons to choose three plays and said, "The record in D-six was too cracked to play so I replaced it with another I had laying around, rather than leave the slot blank. I can pull it if you want." The jukebox plattered the disk as they watched, smooth as silk, and out from the machine's speakers spilled the voice of Elvis Presley crooning "Return to Sender."

I gave a letter to the postman
He put it in his sack
Bright and early next morning
He brought my letter back

Handy waited for a reaction, saw the two alleged brothers share a look, followed by a smile.

"Elvis. That's cool," the younger one said. "Thanks."

Handy let the next two records play, finishing up his demo, and killed the generator. He handed an invoice over to Jay and said, "Total comes to just under what I quoted: seven-forty, even. Minus your two-hundred-dollar deposit, you owe me five-forty."

The white man gave the invoice a cursory glance, passed it over to his brother. "Well, I don't know. That seems kind of high."

Handy set his feet and suppressed a deep sigh. He hated being right about shit like this. "It's what we agreed upon. Less, even."

"Yeah, but..." Vince grinned. "Eight hundred bucks for an old piece of junk like this. How about you give us a break on the labor?"

"What kind of break?"

"Three-hundred dollars," Jay said. "We give you two-forty now and call it even. I think that's fair, don't you?"

Handy studied the two men evenly, weighing them for bluster versus actual malice, and concluded the difference hardly mattered. They were his junior by fifteen years, at least, and would probably send him to the hospital just by putting a hand to his chest. This wasn't an argument he could win.

"Give me the two-forty."

The man named Jay counted it out in cash and slapped it into Handy's open hand. Hard.

"Pleasure doing business with you."

Quincy gave Handy a hard time all the next day.

"If you knew that was gonna happen—"

"I didn't know anything. I had a strong suspicion, that's all."

"You need to call the cops."

"And tell them what? That I got gypped out of three hundred dollars on a service call? It's a civil matter, Quincy, not a criminal one."

"So call your damn lawyer and sue the bastards."

"Right. Invest countless work hours and a hundred dollars or so in legal fees to get back three hundred. If I'm lucky. That what you mean?"

"What I mean is, you gotta do *somethin'*. You can't just let 'em do you like that, Handy."

"They didn't do anything to me I didn't let 'em do. I fucked up. It's a lesson learned. Next time I'll just say no."

Or take my Sig Sauer along with me on the return, Handy thought but left unsaid. He was no less enraged by the injustice that had been done to him the night before than Quincy, but hindsight was twenty/twenty and payback didn't seem to be in the offering. Had he been fifteen years younger, he might have been less willing to turn the other cheek, but everything it would take now for him to recover his money from Jay and his brother Vince added up to too much expense for not enough return. He had to let it go and move on.

It was small comfort, but experience had taught Handy that penny-ante hoods like the two white men who had just taken him for a ride never went unscathed for long. Eventually, one hairbrained scheme or another blew up in their faces and all the pain and suffering they had coming caught them right between the eyes.

Sadly, it was highly unlikely Handy would be there to see it when it happened to Jay and his little brother Vince.

Binny paid the ransom.

It caught in his throat like a chicken bone, like burning bile that had started its way up but could not be swallowed back down. The submission, the *ad*mission that the thieves had put him in a spot from which there was no exit except through their demands would not give him rest. But Binny believed them when they said they would destroy the jukebox if he didn't buy it back, and the juke had been a prized possession of his late father. Before its theft, he would have thought himself too hard to care about such things, but he knew differently now. *Binny's* wasn't really *Binny's* without the Seeburg.

So the thieves had called to name their price and tell him how they wanted the three grand paid, and Binny had followed their instructions to the letter and got the jukebox back. He made the drop in one place and recovered the machine later in another—it had been left under a blue tarp in an alley off Marshall Road, bearing a fresh dent or two but otherwise looking none the worse for wear. Beforehand, he had given some thought to calling Deputy Thorn and even more to refusing to cooperate, keep his three thousand dollars and track the jukebox and the thieves down on his own if he could. But a cooler head had prevailed, and he'd paid the ransom instead, and it seemed his capitulation had been rewarded. *Binny's* had its music box back, the legacy of its original owner restored.

Still, Lewis Binny was not a man quick to forget an injury salted by both insult and expense. Weeks after he'd returned the Seeburg to its old spot on the bar's checkered floor, Binny continued to seethe, determined to find out who had robbed him and the limits of their threshold for pain. He remained as convinced as ever that his ex-wife Peoria had been the mastermind of the crime, and he believed her accomplices were patrons of his bar. Not friends, certainly, because Binny didn't really have any, but men who came in to drink his booze and eat his food at least two, three times a month or so. Smiling, laughing, tripping over their feet on their way out the door and back to their little lives of poverty and ignorance.

His list of suspects started with men he either knew or had heard were Peoria's fuck-buddies: Sandy Wells, Cyril Matthews, Jeff Sipes, Andy Butterworth... But this was like saying a bad apple was buried somewhere in a bushel of dozens. Binny didn't know any of these assholes well enough to assess their criminal potential or their disdain for him, beyond a calculated guess that they were all capable of the robbery and extortion he was trying to solve. He could put a gun to Peoria's head to speed things along, sure, but that approach would land him in jail for certain and, worse, could prove to be fruitless, should his ex-wife actually turn out to be innocent of the conspiracy of which he thought her guilty.

No, he'd have to find the bastards without Peoria's help. And it took him weeks to realize how he might do it.

A curiosity in the Seeburg's theft and return that Binny couldn't quite understand was that it had come back to him in better shape than it had been in before it was stolen. It bore the scars of having been dropped on its ass, and yet it remained fully functional, its inner workings running quieter and more precisely than Binny could ever remember them being. Somebody had worked on the juke while it was gone. That was the only possible explanation.

And it occurred to Binny that, if he could find out who this somebody was, he could also find out who had put them up to it.

Handy was replacing a striker on an old Remington typewriter when the phone rang. "Handy's Repairs."

"Yeah, hey. Tell me, you do any work on jukeboxes?"

The word "jukebox" caught Handy's immediate attention.

The guy on the other end of the line sounded agitated, like he'd been making calls like this all day.

"Occasionally. What have you got?"

"I've got a Seeburg." Handy put down the screwdriver he'd been rolling around in his right hand. "You work on Seeburgs?"

"I have. May I have your name, sir?"

"Done any work on one recently? Like, say, about a month ago?"

"Yes. An HF-One Hundred series. Did you lose one?"

The caller was thrown by the question. He was silent for a long moment. "'Lose' ain't exactly the word I would use," he said.

"How about I tell you about my Seeburg and you tell me about yours," Handy suggested.

"Sounds like a good idea. Why don't you go first?"

They traded stories. The guy on the phone was careful to omit all names from his, including his own. When they were done, he said, "I don't know any Jay or Vince, but based on your description, I've got a general idea of who you might be talkin' about."

"And you think they're customers of yours?"

"The two I got in mind are, yeah."

"So what are you planning to do? If you don't mind my asking."

"Actually, I do mind your askin'. And you'll probably be better off not knowin', anyway."

There was no way to know over the phone, of course, but Handy's caller didn't sound like the kind of man who'd have any reluctance about doing serious injury to people who crossed him. Or worse.

"May I make a suggestion?" Handy asked.

"Like?"

"Like you'll want to be sure you've got the right two guys. Before you do anything rash, I mean. And I might know a way you could do that."

Another long pause. "I'm listenin'."

"Have you done anything to the machine since you got it back? Anything at all?"

"Besides plug it in? No."

"Good," Handy said.

Cyril no longer felt comfortable drinking at *Binny's* but Nelson insisted the occasional visit was necessary. Binny might find it odd if they stopped coming in altogether and the safe thing to do, if they wanted their luck to hold, was draw as little suspicion from him as possible.

"Besides. Where else we gonna go?" Nelson asked. This was Stoney Brook Township, after all.

What Nelson wasn't mentioning was the thrill he got out of being at *Binny's* these days, as the brothers were tonight. They'd ripped Binny off not once but twice, and here he was serving them hot wings and beer at their table in the back, forced to treat them like any other customer in the place because for all he knew, that's all they were. And in the background all the while, the barkeep's beloved jukebox played song after song, powerless to warn Binny that its former kidnappers were close enough to touch.

It was beautiful.

Not that Cyril cared. Nothing could improve his mood. By mutual consent, his fling with Peoria was over and the celibacy with which he'd been left to fill the void didn't suit him. Not even Sharon Anderson, the saucy little cashier at the local 7-11, who had invited herself to their table, could bring a smile to Cyril's lips. And God knew, much to Nelson's amazement, she was trying.

"I've never done brothers before," she said at one point, three margaritas into the evening.

That was all Nelson needed to hear. He'd been trying to get a rise out of Sharon for months without success and, with or without Cyril, he wasn't going to let this chance pass him by.

"You want to get out of here?" Nelson asked, reaching for his wallet.

"Yeah, I do," Cyril said.

"I was askin' the lady, dumb-ass." Nelson looked to Sharon.

She smiled, swaying in her seat. "In a minute. After I've heard some Elvis."

"Some what?"

"You know, Elvis? The King? There's just something about his voice that really gets me hot."

Cyril looked at her like a toad that had just hopped onto their table. "Elvis Presley?"

"You think Binny's got any Elvis on that thing?"

Like his brother, Nelson found the sudden intrusion of Elvis Presley into their shapely companion's train of thought highly obnoxious, but getting laid always involved a certain amount of give and take. He started out of the booth, digging into the pocket of his jeans for a quarter.

Later, on their way out to the car in the parking lot, Sharon bolted. Just like that.

"I'm feeling sick. I better go home," she said, drifting out of Nelson's reach before he could stop her. She jumped into her Buick and was gone.

"What the fuck," Nelson said, pissed.

Cyril laughed and tossed his brother the keys to the truck. Binny didn't show himself in the back of the cab until Nelson had started the engine.

"You need to put an alarm in this old piece of shit," he said.

Cyril spun around after he got over the shock, froze like a marble statue when he saw the sawed-off Binny had trained in his general direction.

"Binny! What the hell?"

"Little Rick's closing up for me tonight, while you boys and me go for a ride."

"A ride where?" Nelson demanded.

"I'll tell you on the way." He tapped the front seat at Nelson's back with the snub-nose of the 10-gauge. "Start driving. Unless you like your chances against me and this old girl right here in the cab of this truck."

The brothers didn't. Nelson started driving.

"What the hell's this all about, Binny?" Cyril asked, his voice shaking.

"Three thousand dollars for my jukebox and twenty-five hundred in liquor, more or less. You two are the clowns that robbed my place five weeks ago."

Nelson was having trouble keeping his eyes on the road. "What? Who—"

"You told me. Just now, when you put that song on the box."

"What song? You're crazy!" Nelson said. But Cyril was strangely quiet.

"'Return to Sender'. Elvis Presley. Sharon sat with you boys tonight and asked to hear some Elvis as a little favor to me."

Nelson almost winced. Apparently, he was still waiting for Sharon Anderson to give him a second thought of her own accord. "So I played her an Elvis record. What's that supposed to prove?"

"Nelson!" Cyril shook his head in warning.

"Your brother gets it," Binny said. "There were no Elvis records in that jukebox before it was stolen, dumbass, so he's not on the playlist. But you knew he was in there tonight, and where to find him: D-six."

Now Nelson was as silent as his brother.

"D-six hasn't worked on that machine in eight years and the playlist says so. I marked it 'Out of Order' myself."

Nelson kept driving, trying to think of an explanation that might save them, only to face the sorry fact that no such explanation existed. He'd simply fucked up. *They* had fucked up. From robbing Binny at Peoria's behest to cheating that nigger repairman out of a lousy three hundred dollars, everything he and Cyril had done over the last six weeks had been stupid. Just plain stupid.

"Stupid," he said out loud.

One day not long after Binny took the Matthews brothers out for a ride, Handy White got a package in the mail. Somebody—he thought he could guess who—had sent his old Elvis Presley 45 back, no note included.

But a note hadn't really been necessary. The record's title was message enough.

BIFF'S PLACE

Debra H. Goldstein

Grand-Daddy swore music soothed the soul. His attitude and interpretation were purely clinical. He'd spent years in the university's lab playing music and seeing how it affected mood, blood pressure, and stroke recovery in mice and humans. If he'd lived a little longer, I could have told him about music's impact on murder and murderers.

I wonder what factors he would have considered. Perhaps gender, race, or family background? Maybe he would have added time and type of murder or weapon of choice. No matter how many elements he considered, knowing him, Grand-Daddy would have concluded the sampling was too small to be relevant.

That might have been the one time we disagreed. When it comes to murder, I believe a factor of one is sufficient for analysis. That's why my research, now that I work at the university, has veered in a different direction than his. He believed in examine, test, and repeat for certainty, while I lean more toward psychological profiling based upon human characteristics and how different emotional, environmental, and unpredicted events change outcomes.

Some have compared my research to shooting craps. It's doubtful my professional work would please Grand-Daddy, but I know he'd be thrilled if he could hear me jamming on my washboard Saturday nights at Biff's Place.

Grand-Daddy introduced me to Biff's Place in 1962, when I turned ten. Raising me after my parents died, he thought there were certain things that should be part of my education. Biff's Place was one of those things.

The first time he took me there, he told me "Ronnie, there are only a few juke joints like this left." I thought he meant in Mississippi, but he was referring to anywhere.

When he stopped chuckling, he continued his history lesson. "Juke joints were created in the South during the era of the Jim Crow laws, so black sharecroppers and plantation workers had a place to kick back after their long hours of work. Mr. Biff opened Biff's place almost twenty years ago with the idea that it would be a haven where race and social class would be ignored for the sake of the music."

"Have you been coming to this heaven since then?"

Again Grand-Daddy laughed. "I guess heaven is the right word. And yes, I have. Some of the best jazz and blues musicians play here, so I come to hear them. There's something about their music that I can't find in the lab."

He whistled as we drove through a neighborhood that had houses a lot smaller than his or the one where I used to live. Each time he turned on a street, I tried to read its sign. D Street was the last one I read before he said, "Here we are."

I glanced out the window, looking for the juke joint. I wasn't quite sure what it would look like, but I knew I didn't see it. The only things on D Street were a few rundown houses. The owner of one of them seemed to have tried to disguise its peeling paint by stringing a few Christmas lights across its roof and front doorway. Otherwise, it looked like any of the other two-story houses on the block.

"Where's the music place?"

"Right in front of you."

All I saw was the Christmas-light house and a lot next to it filled with cars.

"Are you sure we're on the right street?"

"Yes." He pointed toward the driveway.

My gaze followed the direction of his finger. This old house sure didn't look like the auditorium where Mama took me to see *The Nutcracker*.

"You're teasing me." I crossed my arms and didn't move.

"You'll see." He got out of the car, walked around to my side, opened my door, and offered me his hand. Still believing he was pulling my leg but not sure why, I took his hand and let him lead me down the gravel driveway.

I heard faint sounds ahead of us. About halfway down, I recognized the notes of a song. I didn't know what to think until we got to where the driveway wound behind the house, and there I saw musicians playing their hearts out under a tin roof that covered a three-walled wood platform that served as their stage. Even though I was only ten, it was at that moment I realized this might be Mr. Biff's home, but it was also something special. Not only were all types of people sitting at tables, enjoying the blues and jazz, but some were dancing with abandon on a small wooden dance floor set just below the front of the stage.

To this day, I remember staring at the people on and off the dance floor. My surprise and lack of understanding were all summed up by the tone in which I asked, "Grand-Daddy?"

"I told you it was a place for everyone to enjoy good music. They've also got great ribs. Want some?"

Before I could answer, he led me toward a big open fire with spits of meat turning above it. A man even larger and rounder than Grand-Daddy stood to its side, holding tongs and handing people ribs wrapped in aluminum foil. "Junior, this is my granddaughter Ronnie. Ronnie, this is Mr. Biff's son Junior."

He smiled at me. I was so fixated by his size and his beautiful midnight skin, I couldn't mumble anything except "thank you" when he handed me a foil-wrapped package. After thanking Junior more properly by paying him for my ribs, Grand-Daddy ushered me to a table on the far side of the dance floor. He opened the packet for me and, with jazz nourishing my soul, I bit into Junior's ribs. They were the best I'd ever tasted.

In between bites, a hand grasped my shoulder. I turned to see a slight man with a grin as wide as Junior's. For such a small person, his grip was strong. "You must be Ronnie. Your Grand-Daddy's mighty proud of you."

I looked from him to Grand-Daddy, not quite sure how to react. "Thank you, sir. I'm proud of him, too."

Apparently, this was my evening to amuse grown-ups, because both Grand-Daddy and the man laughed. "You should be."

"Now, Biff," Grand-Daddy said. Realizing this must be Mr. Biff, I snuck a quick peek at Grand-Daddy. He looked pleased as punch.

I guess he was so excited that his manners went out the window because he didn't introduce me to Mr. Biff. Instead, I took matters into my own hands. I thrust my sticky hand out at Mr. Biff. He shook it.

"Pleased to meet you, Mr. Biff. Grand-Daddy said your place is like heaven and that he enjoys coming here, so I'm sure I will, too."

"Well, let's see that you do. Come with me."

I glanced at Grand-Daddy for permission. His nod was almost imperceptible, but it was a yes. With Grand-Daddy staying behind, Mr. Biff led me through the dance floor to the stage. My forty-two pounds didn't seem to matter to him as he swung me onto the stage. He scrambled up beside me and said something to the two guitarists already sitting there.

Leaning over to where a group of instruments lay, Mr. Biff picked up two washboards. He handed me the smaller one, plus a wooden spoon, and then put metal thimbles on his fingers. "Ronnie, when I nod to you, I want you to hit your spoon against your washboard. Understand?"

I don't know if he heard my whispered "yes," because the guitarists began playing. Holding his washboard to his chest, Mr. Biff tapped and scraped his metal board, complementing the beat, much like a drum. Periodically, he nodded to me and I diligently struck my spoon against my washboard. When we finished the number, everyone applauded. I left the stage in a cloud of euphoria.

It was a high that I haven't often achieved since then. In the years since my first visit, Grand-Daddy passed, I've grown up, and the world and politics have changed, but not the atmosphere at Biff's Place. It's still going strong every Saturday night. Oh, and Junior's ribs are still the best in town.

There have been some changes, though. Not all of them to my liking. Somewhere in the last decade, Mr. Biff has stopped sitting to the side of the stage, playing at least one set where he improvised beautiful guitar riffs. Instead, he has settled into using his guitar or slide trombone to warm up the crowd, or when the other musicians take a break. Most evenings, he simply works the crowd—welcoming everyone. Whether he clasps a hand, smiles, or poses for a photograph with an out-of-town guest, Mr. Biff is still the heart of Biff's Place.

There's talk he's slacking off because he's given up some of the administrative duties, like setting the lineup for the acts or collecting money, but he's earned the right. After all, he's ninety-two now.

For his ninetieth birthday and the celebration honoring forty years of Biff's Place, the local paper sent out a young reporter to do an article commemorating both. I happened to sit with them during the interview, so I heard how the cub tried to find a way to sensationalize his story.

Mr. Biff wasn't having any of it.

When the reporter tried stirring something up by commenting on integration and the dance floor, Mr. Biff cut him off. "We don't have no color here. If you bring a bottle of wine or a couple of beers and pay your ten dollars, you're welcome to grab a seat, mosey around, or dance the night away. People come here for the music, but if you get hungry, you can get an order of BBQ ribs from my son."

Trying a different tactic, the young man observed that Mr.

Biff let newcomers sit in with established players. Surely, the reporter said, "that isn't fair to patrons who pay their cover charge expecting to hear only name talent."

That one absolutely made Mr. Biff guffaw. When he finally got himself under control, he stared at the kid. "How else they going to know what greatness is? They not only learn from the masters, but they don't want to be shown up, so they go home and practice twice as hard."

Mr. Biff not only believed in practice and learning from the best, but he was adamant that he wouldn't put up with any nonsense at Biff's Place. He'd seen his share of drugs and other such in the music world and had decided that wasn't going to be tolerated at Biff's Place. People weren't there to do drug deals, carouse, or start fights. To quote my Grand-Daddy misquoting some politician, "It's the music, stupid."

At least it was from the forties through the seventies. The seventies brought a new generation of neighbors to D Street and the surrounding neighborhood. These folks weren't as educated about Biff's Place and its cultural significance. Instead, they complained about the cars, traffic, and noise. A few brought their issues directly to Mr. Biff, but when his response didn't satisfy them, they took it to County Sheriff Thomas Jefferson Riley.

Better known as T.J., the sheriff has never been one to turn a blind eye to a problem. That's why, by 1970, he'd been repeatedly elected county sheriff. The last time, the other party didn't even run a candidate against him. They knew T.J. was in it for the long haul, and that, in Mississippi, there's no set limit to the number of years a sheriff can serve.

As he did with any citizen's complaint, T.J. apparently listened sympathetically and promised to do something about the cars roaming the neighborhood looking for Biff's Place. Understanding the optics of pleasing folks, he did. T.J. immediately had big signs made with arrows and words pointing the way to Avenue D and Biff's Place.

The next Saturday night he rode through the neighborhood,

stopping here and there to post the signs. T.J. was so efficient that he was always right on time for his weekly saxophone solo at Biff's Place.

He'd been playing there for years, but most people, unless they frequented Biff's Place often, didn't realize it because T.J. was white, and back then, blacks and whites seldom sat down together. But behind the scenes, the magic of music broke those barriers.

Until Grand-Daddy died, he, T.J., and Mr. Biff were tight. I remember Grand-Daddy observing that T.J. was Mr. Biff's son from another mother. While T.J. might make some noise here and there, it was a safe bet he would never shut Biff's Place down.

The signs didn't stop people from crowding the street, parking on the edge of yards, or making noise, but they proved T.J. had responded to the public's complaints.

I saw the signs, but I didn't pay much attention to them. I wasn't going by Biff's Place as often as I had in the past. Even if the summer of 1970 hadn't been the kind where the sweltering Mississippi heat took care of the need for any kind of cover or clothes at night, I was, at eighteen, so hot to trot, I didn't need to look at a thermometer. I'd found the one special boy, Cooper "Skip" Carter, with whom I wanted to spend the rest of my life.

Mr. Biff didn't like him.

That was okay with us. My twenty-two-year-old love didn't care to spend Saturday evenings at Biff's Place anyway. His music tastes ran more to hard metal than jazz or blues.

Coming from the way Grand-Daddy had raised me, Skip's bad-boy image excited me.

"Look," he'd told me. "I bounced in and out of college and got into trouble for some stupid pranks." He rubbed his left thumb against the second and third fingers of his hand. "Luckily, my old man had the bank account to make that crap go away."

One of the nights we were riding around in his truck, I mentioned how close Mr. Biff, T.J., and Grand-Daddy had been. Skip frowned and spat out the window. "I did a stint in rehab last year because of our no-good local sheriff."

"T.J.?"

"Yeah, him. He didn't like my friends, always hassling them and hassling me just because I was with them. One time he arrested us for drug possession, but he couldn't prove I had anything on me. He charged me just the same, then convinced my father that a stint in rehab would be the best way for me to walk away with a clean record. I don't blame the old man for thinking rehab was better than a chance of probation or jail time, but T.J.'s at the top of my shit list. All those sessions examining who I really am were the biggest pile of garbage imaginable. The only benefit of that place was I learned a lot of practical things, including who I can trust."

He kissed me and I melted. So what if he'd been a wild child? It was all behind him. Once this summer ended, Skip planned to start a two-year program at our local community college before transferring to Ole Miss.

I was ecstatic. We'd be in lock step at the junior college, where I was going to work toward an associate degree. Until I'd met Skip, I'd assumed I'd follow the traditional route from junior college to a four-year school to receive a college degree. It was something Grand-Daddy had encouraged before he died. But who knew now? Where would our dreams take us?

Lying entwined in bed, we often talked about making a future together. One thing Skip wanted to do was travel. "You know," he said, "we're at an age that if we put off school for a year, we could see the world fairly cheaply by staying at youth hostels. You've never been to Europe, have you?"

"I've never been out of Mississippi."

He let go of me and propped himself up on our pillows. "Then, that's what we need to do. The Alps in Switzerland, gondola rides and The Leaning Tower of Pisa in Italy, and, of course, Paris, the city of love. Doesn't that sound wonderful?"

It did. I was sure Grand-Daddy would have understood that four years is a long time to wait when you're in love. We decided to go in the fall, but in the meantime, we vowed to make the most of our summer in Mississippi.

Trips to the lake, picnics, odd jobs for him, and a schedule of sleeping in and staying up late made the days and nights speed by. The only time Skip left my side was for an occasional day of squirrel or raccoon hunting—the two animals Mississippi legally allowed him to shoot in the summer. On those days, I prayed he'd come home empty-handed. Neither the idea of his shooting an animal, even a squirrel or raccoon, nor the idea of eating it sat well with me.

Skip tried to interest me in hunting with him, but when that didn't work, he suggested shooting might be something we could do together. Going to the dresser, he pulled out a pistol like those I'd seen on TV.

"I didn't know you had a gun in there."

He gently rubbed the gun's shiny chrome finish. "This is my pride and joy. It's a Colt 1911 .45 caliber."

"Please be careful. It looks like it could go off easily."

"Relax. This baby has a feather trigger, but the safety is on."

Even if the safety was on, I wasn't comfortable with the way Skip casually handled his gun. The tension in my shoulders only eased when he put it back into the drawer.

As the summer progressed, we rock 'n' rolled along, avoiding blues and jazz. Everything was perfect as we made our plans for the fall. Perfect that is until Skip came home agitated and out of sorts after a day of hunting.

Hoping to relax him, I rubbed his back. After a few minutes, his mood seemed to lighten. "Better?"

He turned toward me, put his hand under my chin, and raised my face to see his clearly. "You're right, babe. No need to be gloomy. Let's go out and have ourselves a night on the town. Put on that pretty dress of yours and we'll have dinner at Joe's."

For a moment I thought about the special chicken cacciatore dinner I'd planned for us, but seeing Skip's eagerness to please me, I agreed.

"Give me a minute to change and put away what I have in the oven."

"Sure thing." Skip leaned over, kissed me, and mumbled something about an appetizer.

We left for dinner a little later than we'd planned. While I got in the front seat of the truck, he grabbed two beers out of a Styrofoam cooler on the floor of the backseat. Getting in next to me, he made a grand gesture of twisting the cap off the first and handing it to me. As I giggled at his formality, Skip opened the second and drank half in one swig.

I raised my eyebrows.

"It's okay, babe. I've got this under control."

I snuggled closer to him.

He turned up the volume on his radio. A few minutes later, Skip turned the car into the almost-empty parking lot of a convenience store a couple of blocks from Biff's Place.

I raised my head from his shoulder.

"Sorry, I need to make a quick business call before we go to dinner." Skip pointed to the pay phone at the end of the building. "Stay in the car. This will only take a moment."

"But—"

"Don't worry. I'll leave the motor and radio on. Plus, you'll have my special friend with you." He reached under the seat and pulled out the gun he'd shown me in our bedroom a few weeks earlier. I knew Skip usually kept his hunting rifle secured in the back of his truck, but I had no idea this pistol was hidden here, too.

"Isn't it illegal to have that in here?"

"You worry too much."

He flicked something on the side of the gun then handed it to me.

I took it carefully. "The safety?"

"I don't want you having to deal with that if you need it. This baby's cocked and locked, ready to fire. You'll be okay while I make my call." When Skip slammed the door, I stared at the gun, frightened the jarring bang might set it off.

Grand-Daddy had taught me lots of things, but guns were never in his lesson plans. One part of me wanted to put the pistol down, while the other counted the seconds for Skip to return and take it from me.

Hearing a voice shouting, I gingerly, lest I moved too fast because the gun's safety was still off, glanced around the parking lot. The person yelling stood in the store's doorway.

"Turn that racket off or get out of here before I call the police!"

Afraid to reach for the radio knob, I didn't respond, but neither did Skip, who was talking on the phone, his body turned away from the man in the doorway. After a few seconds, the man turned and went back inside the store.

Skip was still on his call. Finally, he hung up and sauntered back to the truck.

He slid behind the steering wheel and slammed it with the palm of his hand, his gaze scanning the parking lot.

"Let's go, please. The man in the store said if we didn't turn down the music, he'd call the police."

Skip hit the steering wheel again. "Not now. Just sit there and be quiet. There's some business I have to take care of first."

With my head, I motioned toward the gun. "Don't you want to put this back under the seat?"

"In a minute. I might need it."

"What?"

"Only kidding. Lighten up a bit." He hushed as a car entered the parking lot. It drove toward us, blinking its lights once. When our lights went off and then back on, I realized that Skip had responded. The other car drove up next to us, driver to driver, making it easy for the drivers to talk.

Without a word, the other driver held up a clear plastic bag. Skip nodded and reached under his seat again. I flinched, waiting to see if he had another gun. Instead, he pulled out a brown paper bag. When Skip partially opened the bag to expose its contents to the other driver, I could see the bag was filled with money.

Just like that, the bags were switched, the exchange completed. Skip casually dropped the plastic bag on the seat between us. As a few pills escaped onto the seat, the other driver backed up and sped out of the parking lot.

We sat there, our music still blaring. The same man again came out of the store, threatening to call the police if we didn't turn down the music.

Skip laughed. He flipped a bird at the man but showed no inclination to move. The screamer went back inside the store.

"Please, let's do what he asked or let's go." I looked down at my trembling hands, which still held the gun, and willed them to stop moving.

"All in good time. It drives him crazy to have music blaring in his parking lot."

"You've done this before?" I didn't need an answer. I didn't know the man I was sitting next to. Still holding the gun, I reached for the car door handle as a police car came into the parking lot. It parked near the entrance of the store.

"Where do you think—" Skip yanked me back into the truck and took the gun from my hand as the driver climbed out of the police car. It was T.J.

Instead of going into the store, T.J. walked across the lot in our direction, his hand resting on his holster. "Hey, there," he called. "Turn down the music, please."

I reached for the radio's button, but Skip swatted my hand.

"Come on, Skip. Let's get out of here."

"I don't think so. I'm tired of that pig always putting his nose into my business. Maybe it's time to teach him a lesson." He trained the gun on T.J.

"Skip, no!"

"Be quiet."

Ignoring me huddled in the seat next to him, Skip waited, chanting, "Bang, Bang, you're going to be dead." I tried to warn T.J., but only a squeak came out of my mouth. Even if I had been able to yell, I doubt T.J. would have heard me, but the man sitting next to me did. He stopped aiming his gun long enough to slap me and say, "Shut up."

Cowering, I couldn't silence a soft whimper.

His hand darted at me again, but by now, I was just outside his reach.

T.J. approached the truck, repeating his suggestion to turn down the music. Skip didn't answer.

It was only when T.J.'s eyes and mouth opened in surprise as he simultaneously stared down the barrel of the gun and began to duck, that I reacted. I brought my left hand down hard against Skip's arm, much like a karate chop I'd seen on television. The sound of a blast, a scream and silence filled my ears.

I sat still, absorbing the slack of his jaw, empty eyes, and the red splotch spreading across his stomach. I started to reach across the seat, hoping to slow the flow, when T.J. opened the passenger door and stopped me.

"He needs help."

"Not now."

T.J. pulled me from the car. "Come on. Get over to Biff's Place. Go in through the front door. It's unlocked."

"What?" In all the years I'd gone to Biff's Place, I'd never been in his house beyond the downstairs bathroom in the back that he let everyone use.

"Ronnie, hush. Just do what I'm telling you to do. I'll try to call Mr. Biff and warn him you're coming, but if I don't get him, wait in the kitchen. He'll come in to cool off between sets. Tell him I said to clean you up and get you on stage with your washboard."

I stared at him. "But..."

"Do it. Now!"

Without another word, I followed his instructions. I ran the two blocks like the wind. I found Mr. Biff already in the kitchen. He led me to a chair and without a word he washed my hands and face. "Take off your blouse."

"What?"

"You've got blood on it." I glanced down and saw blood spatter on my shirt. I fought the urge to retch by focusing on easing out of my shirt and sliding into the Biff's Place T-shirt that Mr. Biff handed me.

"Stand up."

I did as I was told.

"You'll do. Now, come on." Still carrying my blouse and the washcloth, now wadded into a ball, he led me outside. "Get on stage, grab a washboard and jam. Make it fancy."

Again, I followed directions, but I never took my eyes off Mr. Biff as he walked up to Junior and his flaming pit. He said something to Junior and then, taking one of the sticks I'd seen Junior use in preparing his ribs, I saw Mr. Biff drop my shirt and the washcloth into the fire. He poked and prodded at it. From the leap of the flames, I gathered he'd made sure there would be no trace of either.

Looking away, I concentrated on making my washboard sing. When we finished the number, everyone applauded. Although somewhat calmed by the music, I didn't take the lead again for the rest of the evening, I stayed on the stage until T.J. arrived, and he and Mr. Biff motioned me off.

The next few days were a blur. T.J. took me back to the apartment to gather my few belongings, and he found me another place to stay. After the local newspaper learned about the meth-amphetamine in Skip's system and about the hundreds of diet pills found in his truck—diet pills back then included meth as an appetite suppressant—they spun my lover's story as being that of a kid who went to rehab, came home, relapsed, and put himself out of his own misery. No one questioned their conclusion.

There was a mention or two that I'd been seen around town with the deceased, but it faded because, with Mr. Biff and T.J.'s help, I went straight to Ole Miss instead of the junior college. By the time I came home, degrees in hand, not many remembered the incident. Instead, they all were too busy remarking on the cute love of my life, my son. I think Grand-Daddy would also have loved him and understood why now I study how people behave and whether the traits of killers can be inherited.

THE EXCHANGE
Gary Phillips

Santamaria was doing his best to pleasure the younger woman, but he could tell by the expression on her face she was faking it. Oh, he knew he'd been on the ones and twos oral-sex-wise when he'd been servicing her last evening. But now, in the pre-dawn hour of missionary time, he was doing his best to get that long-stroke rhythm going, but it just wasn't like when he was younger. Hell, in those days he could go three times a night like a pile driver, snorting coke off a firm titty and downing half a bottle of bourbon. Things were different now that he was past forty and crashing toward the half-century mark. His jaunty little hoop earring didn't distract from the crow's feet. And these days he was too often dwelling on the past, rather than imagining the future he lamented. Well, at least she wasn't laughing at him, at least not outwardly.

Then it was as if a bolt of electricity snaked up his spine into his shoulders, pulsing through him. The woman's eyes snapped open, a smile animating her face in the half-light. She had great eyes; their cinnamon color is what first attracted him to her. Her grip tightened and the muscles in her legs around his waist got rigid, and damned if she didn't let out a gasp. Now he was grinning as a rocking sensation overtook them and the bed itself began to buck like in *The Exorcist*.

"Oooh, shit, baby," he bellowed as he hit it like a champ

and didn't quit.

They locked lips and tongues and the floor began to sway. Santamaria's books, his two high school sports trophies, and other ephemeral keepsakes began to tumble from their shelves. Car alarms went off and dogs howled. They both climaxed, tumbling out of the bucking-bronc bed, laughing and holding onto each other as an earthquake shook Los Angeles. The window overlooking the street down below cracked and its glass tinkled onto the rug. Santamaria's acoustic guitar, which had been leaning on the nearby wall, now lay on the floor.

"Goddamn," she said, kissing him again, her upper body glossy from sweat.

"I do what I can," he joked.

The Southland has experienced fires, riots, even a pandemic, all unpredictable to lesser or greater degrees. But the region could always rely on an earthquake reminding its inhabitants not to get too complacent. You might make it through those other calamities, but when the ground upon which you walk or drive decides to slip and slide, there's not fuck all you can do is try to ride it out it, Santamaria reasoned.

He also knew from experience that convenience store owners would take advantage of the earthquake and jack up the price of bottled water and other essentials. He didn't know at that moment how he himself would benefit from this natural disaster—notwithstanding the temporary improvement of his lovemaking.

The magnitude 3.8 tremor was centered less than eight miles from Santamaria's apartment in Koreatown. Damages were fairly minimal. There was, though, one casualty of the quake. Kenny "Lomo" Duarte had been asleep in bed when the jolt occurred. Mounted above his slumbering form were two crossed samurai swords. Those bad boys had fallen when the wall trembled, and one of the heavy ivory and iron hilts had knocked him in the head, cracking his skull. Later, the doc who examined him in the emergency room told Lomo until the wound healed, he was going to suffer headaches and might even experience blackouts.

Being a conscientious criminal, Lomo reported this to his boss, Trin Li. Unfortunately, she had lined up a run but didn't want to take the chance that her man was going to have a spell at an inopportune moment. As a consequence, she sought a substitute for Lomo. She first approached three others, all of whom were otherwise engaged, with one of them doing a bid at Mule Creek State Prison. That left Santamaria.

"I won't let you down, Trin," he said, standing before her desk.

Smoke from the cheroot between her fingers rose past her hard-lined face and dissipated on the ceiling of her office in her wholesale toy and puzzle business. This was a legitimate enterprise that was also a front for several illegal activities.

A crimson nail pointed at him, the little cigar dangling from the corner of her mouth as if she were a gunslinger. "No fuck-ups, you hear me? This ain't gonna be Barstow, understand?"

"Yes, ma'am."

Santamaria hit the road in his restored '73 Buick Centurion with the sporty rims and the aftermarket 1980s-era combo cassette/CD deck, travelling from L.A. to the exchange location, a juke joint in Zachary, Louisiana, in East Baton Rouge. When he got to the place, Elmira's Inn, he heard zydeco drifting through the live oaks among which the joint was nestled. He parked on the uneven macadam, weeds sprouting through the cracks. From what he'd gleaned from the Google map he'd studied, there was a swamp not too far away. Further, he'd read it wasn't unheard of to see a gator sauntering through a parking lot or lounging in the middle of a gas station around here.

Earlier, after stretching and working the kinks out of his spine from sitting so long, he'd used a grimy mirror at a rest stop's bathroom and shaved his four days' growth of whiskers. Santamaria wanted to look professional. The crowd in the juke could be heard having a good time.

In the trunk of his car, hidden beneath the speakers, was more than a million and a half in yuan. That was its equivalent in U.S. dollars. This was a test run for Trin Li. Of the several hats she wore, one was a money-laundering broker. In this instance she had a rich client in China who wished to stash his converted dollars in the United States, away from the purview of his government. The yuan would be used to pay a factory on the border that produced chemicals for Big Pharma and in the manufacture of illicit drugs such as meth. Some of the precursors were shipped to drug manufacturers in cities such as Toledo. Other portions went to a cartel manufacturing facility in Juarez, Mexico. Both over- and under-the-counter drugs were sold, and the cash, after proper percentages were raked off, went back to a secret account maintained for the client. Tonight, Santamaria also would collect an advance against the profits in dollars as a sign of good faith.

The two dudes Santamaria was to do business with were new cutouts Trin Li hadn't dealt with before, but they'd offered a very competitive rate and had a pipeline out of Galveston into Mexico. Li was doing this because she had it on good authority the DEA had a hook into her current reliable fellow middleman rep'ing the cartel back home in Monterey Park. She'd worried aloud maybe the middleman had been turned. Risks were always involved with a new dance partner, but it wasn't as if she or Santamaria were babes in the woods.

Getting closer to the door, Santamaria was intoxicated by the smells of lush foliage, smoked meat, sweat, and pheromones. Could be his uncertainty was mixed in here too, he reflected, stepping into the murky interior. The heat was close, clingy. He decidedly didn't want to mess this up. Handling the exchange could be his way back in.

On stage a zydeco band called the Subduers were finishing up a rousing rendition of "Tante Na-Na." The bandleader, the lead accordion player, was on his knees working his instrument like a backwoods reincarnation of Hendrix. He writhed and twitched, his head gyrating all around, yet somehow his straw cowboy hat stayed on his head as he worked the hell out of his instrument. The rubboard player was no slouch either. The spoons in his hands damn near sparking across the metal as he percussed his frottoir.

At the bar, varnished railroad ties lashed together and braced atop corrugated metal, Santamaria got a local IPA in a bottle. Leaning his back to the bar, he enjoyed what remained of the band's set. He'd pushed it the last hundred or so miles, wanting to get here early and scope out the scene. He'd made two laps around the juke before parking. Having an escape route in mind might come in handy. Such precautions had served him well in the past. Age hardly meant wisdom, but experience was the mother of survival.

The band left the low stage and the proprietor, a portly gent in a throwback 1940s-style suit and fedora came to the standing mic. Wiping his face with a handkerchief, he said in a heavy drawl, "The boys here gonna take theyselves a break. But don't y'all go away now, hear? Have a beer or two, on you," he chuckled, the crowd laughing along.

Folks who'd been dancing floated back to the scattering of tables or simply stood and talked. On three of the walls were the requisite posters announcing musical acts. The fourth was reserved for personally autographed photos. He paused at the picture of a beaming, eyeliner-wearing Little Richard at a piano. Enjoying the vibe of Elmira's, he resisted having another beer, knowing he'd better keep sharp. Ten minutes later the two entered. It had been pre-arranged that he'd know them, as one of the men would be wearing a Rams cap, symbolizing L.A. Several people had on Saints caps. Santamaria walked over to introduce himself. Both were white.

"Hey," the taller one said. He was lean and had a Fu Manchu mustache, as if he'd been transported to the juke straight from starring in a 1970s triple-X film. His sandy hair was cropped short on top and full at the nape of his neck.

"All right now," Santamaria said, nodding curtly.

The one in the Rams cap eyed Santamaria for a moment,

then said, "What are you?"

He knew what the dude meant, his race a puzzle as his name and skin tone confused a lot of folks' perceptions.

"Kinda like zydeco," he said.

"Huh?"

"A mixture he means," Fu Manchu said.

Santamaria said, "Can we get on with it?"

"Absolutely," Fu Manchu answered.

"Okay, fine," Rams Cap said, holding up his hands. "I ain't all PC and shit like y'all out there in Cali," he snickered. "Damn."

They went out to the parking area and over to their vehicle, a dark-colored Chrysler 300.

"I'm over there," Santamaria said, pointing with his chin. "The Centurion." Several people were outside as well.

"Why don't you pull closer?" Fu Manchu said.

"For sure." Santamaria walked toward his car, passing the club owner chatting with a couple.

"Evenin'," he said, touching the brim of his hat.

Santamaria returned the greeting. He piloted his Centurion over to the other car. He couldn't get side by side, but near enough, and opened the trunk, the light coming on, illuminating the cavity. In there were two boxed and bolted-down subwoofers mounted toward the rear, pointing upward. His spare tire sat atop the liner as well.

"The cash is in them?" Rams Cap asked, leaning in.

"Not exactly," Santamaria answered. He unlatched a hidden catch and from below a panel dropped from the frame. He bent down and extracted two stuffed nylon equipment bags from behind the bumper.

"Nice," Cap's partner said.

The speakers were meant as a distraction. If he spotted cops on his tail, he'd crank them up and when he was stopped, they'd focus on them. An over-eager sort might even rip out the woofers from the housing as had happened in the past and find nothing. Rams Cap handed Santamaria a duffel of dollars. He closed them into the compartment.

"Good doing business with you," Santamaria said.

"Drive safe." Rams Cap grinned lopsidedly.

In his car Santamaria turned on the radio and tuned in one of those overnight shows catering to conspiracies, alien abductions, and the like.

"I'm telling you, Art," the caller was saying, "they got this flying machine looks like something out of the Terminator, the good old version—not that silly new version they tried to foist on us. The truth is there to be seen. That's why we got us a Space Force, if you know what I mean."

"Oh, I do, friend, I do," Art, the host, affirmed.

Santamaria got a kick out of these goofballs. He slowed, approaching a set of train tracks. Bumping over them, for the first time he noticed the car was lilting slightly. Chuckling along with the program, he hadn't noticed anything wrong until now. He pulled over and got out, flashlight in hand. His left rear tire was clearly going flat, the weight of the car gradually pancaking the rubber under the rim. For a moment he considered he'd driven over glass, his light and hand examining the tire. The coincidence of this scratched at him. He unscrewed the valve stem cap when his cursory inventory produced no cause for the air loss.

"Fuck me," he said softly, his flashlight aimed at the valve stem. The cap off, he could see a heavy tack had been inserted there. With the cap screwed on, the tack would depress the valve mechanism, releasing air. That meant the two had done this. Santamaria reconstructed what went down. When they got to Elmira's, they must have scouted the lot and spotted his car with its California plates. He also figured they had to have hung back, knowing this time of night with fewer cars out, he'd have noticed them following. But they would be coming along as this was the way back to the main highway. The play was to get the jump on him as he changed the tire. Flashlight off, he quickly retrieved the duffel just as he heard a car approach, its headlights off. Fortunately, there was a spread of gravel here on the side of the roadway.

Santamaria plunged through the thick vegetation, thickets scraping at him. He chanced using the light to try to find his footing and received a gunshot for his temerity.

"Goddammit, Liss, don't be so trigger happy. He's probably got a gun."

"Can't let ol' United Nations get too far in, now can we?" Liss of the Rams cap said.

"Shhhh," Fu Manchu whispered.

Santamaria went on all fours, scrambling as fast and as quietly as he could through the thick greenery, minor cuts stinging his face and lower arms. He'd strapped the bag across his torso, the whole of it on his back. He came out of the bushes to find himself among a spread of dead leaves. Looming several yards away was a moonlit forest. But to get into the trees and maybe have a fighting chance to live, he'd have to run across those damn leaves. Turning back wasn't an option.

Santamaria shot twice into the tangle behind him. Turning, he ran as if it were decades ago and he had to get down court to defend the basket. Shots boomed and a round struck his back, sending him sprawling. Fear fueled his body and he practically swam through those leaves, getting to momentary safety in the trees beyond. Sitting against a trunk, trying to calm down, Santamaria touched himself, searching for where the bullet had exited. There seemed to be no blood. He took off the bag of money, and looking closely, saw only one hole in it. The money inside was banded together but not in one big stack. How had that stopped a bullet? No matter, he had to get it together.

Those two couldn't come across the leaves at him because they'd make noise. This meant they'd have to go around. If the situation were reversed, he assumed they'd split up and come at him from two directions to pinch him in. He could run deeper into the woods, but they had chosen this juke probably because one or both of them knew the area and had some sense of where he might wind up. Getting centered, he tried to see if he could get Google maps on his phone but there was no reception. He had been heading west and had run off more or less to the north. That meant they had to come at him from the west and east, or so his operating theory went. Instead of going deeper into the woods, he took off toward the east.

Rams Cap Liss was moving confidently through the woods, coming from the eastern end. He used his flashlight sparingly, figuring Mr. Hollywood was deeper in, running for his high-tone life. He'd come to the swamp, Liss knew, and find that getting around that bog was treacherous. Liss certainly didn't think the city boy would dare enter the water for fear of being gator delight. He kept going and after about three minutes more, paused to lean forward, squinting. Off to the right not thirty yards away—was that a light? He crept closer, sure it wasn't Dutcher. That was the light from a phone, he realized. Fool didn't even turn that function off, probably pissing hisself silly. Trying to call for help out here. He got closer.

"Hello? Hello?" Liss heard him say, the panic barely notched down. "Shit," the mark swore.

A grinning Liss rushed forward, pumping rounds where he estimated his target stood. The phone fell to the ground, but he heard no groan. He stared down at the thing. There was a bullet hole in it, yet the face still glowed. Too late he realized the phone had been nestled in the crook of a branch. His heart quickening he turned, shooting. But Santamaria had circled around him the other way and shot him through the side of his head, the bullet blowing out an eye, killing Liss instantly.

Dutcher had heard the gunfire and halted. He took a count of five, then took his phone out, saw a text message from Liss. They'd been texting to communicate while stalking the bagman.

"Got his ass. Coming at you," the text read.

He walked toward his partner. "Liss?" he called out. "Liss," he repeated, chancing clicking on his flashlight. The crack of twin shots echoing through the trees had him swearing as he dove to the ground, shooting, each man using muzzle flash to try to locate the other. Crawling, he felt pain and knew that bastard had got him in the leg, a bullet in his thigh. He wouldn't bleed out but he would be slowed.

"Motherfuck," he swore, gritting his teeth. He stilled himself, hoping to detect movement from his prey. Nothing. Dutcher decided that he best hightail it back to the car. He got up, his weight on the wound, causing it to leak and the muscle to cramp. He wasn't about to waste time trying to make a tourniquet. Like bum-legged Chester Goode in those ancient *Gunsmoke* shows his dad watched on the old-folks channel, he hobbled as fast as he could to get clear of the woods. He stopped now and then to ascertain whether he was being followed, but as far as he could tell, he wasn't. This only made Dutcher more nervous. He reached the edge of the compact woods, the thicket beyond, and past that the car. He was turned around somewhat and wasn't sure he'd come back to where he and Liss had entered. It was Liss who knew his way around these parts, not him. A map on his phone wasn't going to be any help.

"No choice," he muttered. He had to use his flashlight again, briefly shining its light on the wall of green across from where he was. He stepped out and whirled around at the sound of a footfall, firing his gun. He couldn't detect anything because he was breathing so hard through his mouth. Gulping air, Dutcher wasn't going to risk the light again. He reversed and tore into the shrubbery, plowing through with his arms before his face. He made it out onto the side of the roadway. The car was to his left and he limped to it, gun at the ready.

Santamaria had no idea on how to track someone through these or any other woods, night or day. He wasn't sure his bullets had struck the one called Dutcher but the man had stopped returning fire. He counted to sixty then clicking on his flashlight at arm's length, tossed it away from his body. No shots. Was Dutcher playing possum? He waited some more. Then bending low, went and picked up his light. He blazed its beam back and forth. Nothing. If Dutcher was wounded, he'd head back to his car. That was a big-ass "if" Santamaria determined, but what else did he have to go on? He did know where the road was and headed that way.

Dutcher reached the Chrysler, thanking the fates he'd been the driver. He'd already used the fob to unlock the vehicle, and he opened the door. A few cars drove past but the traffic was sparse. It was then he heard a body coming through the green veil and he fired in the direction of the sound. He didn't care whether there was a witness or whether he hit the man or not. As he got behind the wheel, finger on the push-button ignition, he started the car and turned on the lights. As he turned the wheel to get back on the road proper, he checked the sideview mirror for oncoming lights. When he looked back through the windshield, a flashlight came on, temporarily blinding him. He'd put his gun in his lap but as he instinctively turned to get out of the light, the gun slipped off onto the floormat.

"Shit on a stick," he said as he tried to reach down for his gat while keeping an eye on the road. The light had gone out. The gun slid under the seat as he righted the car.

"Oh, fuck me," he yelled, trying to drive and feel under the seat. By necessity he was creeping along.

He collided with something and looking up again, saw it was the rear end of the Centurion. He had to use both hands to reverse and steer. The bumper on the vintage car seemed untouched. Stopping to shift back into drive, he looked around frantically in the dark. Shifting his gaze from the windshield to the driver's side window, Dutcher's last notion in this life was that he wasn't surprised when a muzzle appeared against the glass. The bullets fired from the gun blew out the window and his brains. Dead foot dropping off the gas pedal, the car was nonetheless in gear and continued rolling. But Santamaria caught up with the vehicle and turned it off. He heard another vehicle approaching and quickly got into the car, shoving the cooling Dutcher onto the floor on the passenger side.

A man in a pickup truck came along and glared at Santamaria sitting in the 300 by the side of the road, window down even though it wasn't that warm a night. He slowed and Santamaria let him stare at his profile. The driver kept going. Santamaria popped the trunk and walked back there to get the money.

"Fuck me," he said quietly. The trunk was empty. No secret latch or hidden compart he determined after a hasty search. He closed the Chrysler's trunk and changed his tire on his car. Thereafter he ripped a piece of Dutcher's shirt off and stuffed the rag in the spout of the gas tank. He lit it and drove away. At some point he'd have to get rid of his gun but not now. The phone Liss had shot was a burner and he had it in his pocket. He'd get rid of it later as well. There were witnesses who'd seen the three of them together but there was nothing to be done about that. He wasn't coming back here. He heard the blast and in his rearview mirror, saw the orange and red cloud of burning gas light up the night like atomic neon when the Chrysler 300 exploded, destroying any trace evidence.

Santamaria was wrong. He did go back to Elmira's. Two nights later, following the double-cross. But this time not to enjoy the music. This time it was after the last hookup had traipsed away and the broken beer bottles swept up. Thereafter the portly proprietor entered his office, leaning a broom and dustpan against the wall. The man from California stepped out of the dark and wrapped the low-E steel-guitar string around the man's sweaty neck. He yanked both ends hard, causing the man to rear back and his hat to fall from his head.

"Sweet...Jesus," he gasped.

Santamaria talked into his ear. "Well cousin, you might be on your way to see the Savior sooner than you intended if you don't give me back my money." He eased off the pressure a degree.

"I don't know what—" he began and got choked off as the string was pulled tighter again.

"Don't bother. It took me a minute to put it together, but there was no other place your partners could have left the scratch between here and coming to kill me. Bet you're the one who did that tack trick." He twisted the steel string. "Now open that floor safe and get those crisp yuans out of it."

The owner did so. Santamaria also took some dollars from in there, too. He'd gotten rid of his gun but had a knife tucked behind his belt in case the owner got frisky.

"For my inconvenience," he said, shaking the banded stacks. He then tied and gagged the man, telling him, "I know you ain't gonna say nothing to the cops, putting the spotlight on your illicit activities and all. I saw some pesos in there. Y'all done this before, probably a couple of bodies disappeared in those woods. Now once word gets out, you about to be in a passel of trouble." He winked at the man who glared back at him wide-eyed, pleadingly shaking his head back and forth.

Outside in the cooling night, he loaded the goods in his trunk. The duffel with the one hole was in there as well. The round had been stopped right in Ben Franklin's left eye. It was partially flat, and Santamaria concluded it must have ricocheted off a tree mostly spent when it entered the bag. Whatever, he hadn't messed this up. It wasn't a replay of Barstow. Taking off, he put in an Albert King cassette tape. When he started singing "Crosscut Saw" about cutting your wood so easy and saying hot dog, he flashed on that cinnamon-eyed chick. He wasn't going to need no earthquake roll when next he saw her. No sir.

WHISKEY RIVER

Trey R. Barker

"Daddy?" I stood in the doorway of the two-room trailer, grocery bag still in my hand, fear wrapping me like a flurry of grace notes off a guitar solo.

"Hiya, Taz, we got some fans here. Can you beat that? In time for dinner."

The tall, bald man nodded. "Stopped to see ol' Dads, maybe hear him play."

"Hell, yeah, I can do that." Daddy turned his chair until his lap steel was directly in front of him. "Whiskey river...take my mind...."

Tomato Red, born Cotton Niebank, had rounded the corner of eighty years old last week, but the bows and the long, slow, final curtain call had started years ago. Some days he was fine, other days angry and violent, but most days all he could manage was to relive his music.

"Don't let her memory torture me...."

A second guy stood silent near Daddy, the gun jammed in his waistband, obvious.

"Friends of Stones?"

The bald man grinned. "He was wondering if you'd come by. Says you got twenty-thousand things to catch up on."

Daddy kept grooving to the Willie tune. It was one of his favorites. He wasn't plugged in, but the notes were clear in the

121

thick East Texas air.

"Funny, I only remember twelve-thousand things," I said.

"Ten years silence breeds interest."

The humidity boiled and I wondered how they'd found us this deep in the choking kudzu and lonely despair of Uncertain, Texas.

Loud, like he was shouting over a rattly band in a small club, the second guy said to my father, "You was any good, you'd'a been on the Grand Old Opry."

The playing stopped. "I was. Four times." Daddy swung an old man's fist into the guy's balls.

Surprised, but unhurt, the guy fell back. He came back quick, his gun out. The bald man stopped him.

"Old man fucking hit me."

"Pussy." Daddy's laugh was bright and sassy. "Started playing clubs when I was fifteen. Guns don't scare me."

The guy put two rounds into Daddy's lap steel guitar. Daddy yelped and fell away from the guitar. When he stood, frail and weak, he said, "Children ought not play with guns."

"Daddy, please," I said. I turned to our visitors. "He's old and having a bad day. Plus, he doesn't have anything to do with this crap."

"No, but he's damned good leverage." The bald man clapped Daddy on the shoulder. "Our friend heard you were looking for Kittery."

Daddy frowned. "You know Kittery? He was in my band. Tomato Red and Lovey."

"I know, buddy. You guys were great. I heard you a few times."

Daddy sat, the shot-up steel guitar forgotten. "Yeah? Like what you heard?"

"Hells to the yeah, buddy. Anyway, Stones figures while you're on your way to see Kittery, you might as well stop and talk things over."

"No idea what you're talking about. Don't even know where

Kittery is."

I'd called all over the Gulf Coast and Texas, New Mexico, and Oklahoma, some places in Arizona, California—all the places Daddy and Kittery had played—to see if anyone had heard anything about Kittery in the last few years. Since I'd come off the road and packed my drums away for good, I'd lost touch with the circuit.

Every call had been a waste of time. No one knew anything. Never occurred to me that Stones would hear about my calls and come sniffing. I'd been hidden so long out here I'd assumed he'd written me off.

But now, two men breathing violence on my father told me differently.

The bald man gave me a predator's snarl. "Zach City, man, where else? Got himself a trailer, courtesy of Stones. Singing at a club, getting his chops back. Got a record deal—"

Daddy laughed. "Horseshit. Ain't nobody gonna produce him without me. Fucker can sing like the angels, but without me? A drunk smokehound. I kept him singing and outta jail."

"Gotta do a better job next time."

"Meaning?"

The bald man waved away my question. "Couple days to go see Stones. After that—" He nodded toward Daddy. "Gotta do what I gotta."

"Come back here again? I'll blow your balls off and watch you bleed to death," I told him.

Again with his grin. "Killah."

When they were gone, headed toward Marshall, my heart started again. I sat next to Daddy, stared at his shot-up instrument—he had five or six more stored away—and tried to breathe through the adrenaline dump.

"That rat-bastard Kittery. The fuck he steal my tapes? I want them back. They all I got left. You and those tapes. Ain't a damned other thing."

I kissed his forehead. "Don't worry, Daddy, I'll get them. I know where he is now."

I fixed him a couple of PB&Js and threw some beer in the fridge. "Make sure you eat. I'll be back tomorrow. Next day latest. There're a couple'a cold burgers in there, too."

If the only way to Kittery—and Daddy's tapes—was through Stones?

No problem.

Then I grabbed the only thing I had worth any money—my Kimber .45.

No fucking problem at all.

Three hours later, in Corsicana, I stopped at the Hitchin' Post.

One of Daddy's old places; a constant stop. One of my favorite clubs, though Dorothy rarely hired any of my bands.

For decades, Tomato Red and Lovey played everywhere, from festivals with ten thousand to tiny roadhouses that sold homebrew distilled through used skivvies or recycled cheap women from man to man to man. I'd played some of these places, too, with eight or ten different bands. Difference 'tween me and Daddy? He played those joints and moved up. I played those joints and then played them again. And again, and again.

But the Hitchin' Post was my first time. It deflowered me. Just a juke joint, old and beat-up, blood stains everywhere but somehow classy for all that. A short bar and a few tables radiating off the bar's front, shaped like a good poker hand. A dance floor that led to a tiny, raised area for the band. Low ceiling, record covers on the walls, mostly signed. Black-and-white publicity photos with men banging conked hair and women beneath slicked-back pixie cuts.

Same as it ever was, except this afternoon it was quiet.

"Who you, white boy?" The bartender resembled a fire hydrant, his voice broken glass.

"I'm looking for Dorothy."

"Don't know no Dorothy."

I whistled. "I sure do. We got tight one night right here, shot for shot through a whole bottle of her homemade. Went home with her. Still my best night ever."

The barman glared. "You gonna disrespect her in fronna me? Get the fuck outta here."

"No woman I respect more." I popped down a Hamilton. "Whiskey. Straight up."

"Asshole." But the money disappeared and almost magically quick he served me the whiskey, trailed by three singles in change.

Warmed by the whiskey, memories stomped all over my mental drum set. Some were mine, but most were Daddy's. Tomato Red making his lap steel weep and wail while Lovey made everyone believe in life and then the afterlife and then something beyond that. Daddy used a pitted whiskey pint bottle for a slide, and it carved every note as beautifully as a soul from the heavens. Kittery sang honey-smooth, velvet and seductive, but he could also shout a greasy blues that could peel the rust off your soul.

I squeezed the whiskey glass. Tomato Red and Lovey had had that intangible something I'd never had. They played sold-out bars and clubs and had a following on the festival circuit. Good reviews and people excited about when they might tour again. Me? I couldn't get paid to give money away. Backed them up a few times on stage, but never shone in the same spotlight.

"Breaking my glass would be a waste of good whiskey."

"Dorothy."

The same soft smile, same bright eyes. She kissed my cheek. "Taz."

I squeezed her hand. "I've missed you."

"But not enough to come see me?" A gentle tease, but with an edge of truth beneath it.

"I've been remiss."

"You're forgiven. You have good reason to stay low."

"Stones."

"Shoulda just killed his ass instead'a breaking all his slot machines."

"What can I say? I thought I should get paid."

Dorothy laughed. "Stones ain't never paid honest in his life."

"Woulda been good information to have *before* the tour."

He'd hired my second band, Growl, to play all his tonks from South Carolina to Bakersfield, California. Our biggest tour ever. But lukewarm reviews and almost zero merch sold. When it was over? Stones shorted us money and I came unglued on some of his money-making slot machines. I managed to flee before his mooks could get the slot machine off of him.

Dorothy nodded toward the bandstand. "No band tonight. The house kit is up there."

When I was sixteen years old and devastatingly shy except behind my drums, Dorothy had let me play. I'd walked away from school at fourteen and started going to all of Daddy's gigs. Dorothy had seen me tapping hands on my thighs while Tomato Red and Lovey played one night and took me to the bandstand during their break so I could play along with the jukebox.

"Remember that applause?" she asked.

"Remember just about pissing myself."

From then on, I played as Mr. Memorial and got paid hard cash. Only played a few gigs with them, though. Kittery said I wasn't up to their level. I walked out before Daddy had to make that choice and started my own thing.

But those playing days were ten years gone, bloody and dead in Stones's place. Couldn't get a gig after that—no offers, no money, nothing. He dried it all up when he put the word out.

"Been a while since I played. I miss it, though. Damn. You know I've been taking care of Daddy?"

Melancholy washed across her mocha-colored face. "I heard a rumor. Hoped it wasn't true. I'm sorry. He's such a good man. Such an incredible musician. He could play the panties off'a any woman he wanted."

"Taught me everything I know, too, 'cept when I do it, women put their panties back on."

"I didn't."

The barman coughed and ran a towel hard and fast through highball glasses.

"He's at the end of his set, Dorothy. Maybe a couple weeks? A month at the outside."

We drank through a moment of silence.

"What do you need, Taz?"

I finished my whiskey, took a deep breath, and said, "I've got some master recordings. You could package them and put them out. Not just my first two albums, but all the outtakes, plus five Tomato Red appearances."

Interest flickered on her face. "He was on those? I don't remember that."

"Producer and record company didn't want those songs. Said why tie myself down to a regional player when they were going to push national."

"Well, that was stupid."

"Stupid is as I did. I went along."

"Now they're out of business, the records are out of print, and you're trying to sell me masters I can't use."

"Come on, Dorothy, you've produced records before. Brand new, never-before-heard songs featuring Tomato Red? They're a goldmine."

Her eyes were so sad. "They're wonderful, I'm sure, but nobody remembers Tomato Red no more. The diehards, maybe, but there's no money there. You had to know that, so what are you doing here?"

I hesitated. "Kittery."

Dorothy sucked her teeth. "That stupid tape? Jesus Christ. Never seen anything cause such a bullshit ruckus between two men. Woulda been better if that tape had never existed."

"That tape was Daddy's best thing."

Her face was as sad as Sunday night alone in a quiet bar. "Cotton Niebank, steel guitarist extraordinaire, and Barney Kessel, greatest jazz guitarist ever."

"No records, no concerts, no agents or crowds or expectations."

"Just two musicians. As pure as music gets."

I grinned. "Well, one mentor-slash-hero and one student-slash-acolyte. Daddy grew up on jazz, Dorothy. He played blues and country, but his soul is...hell, his soul is major sevenths and minor elevenths. Altered dominants."

She took a deep breath. "So you want that tape back."

"Before he dies."

"Kittery ain't still got it."

"Maybe not, but I have to find out."

She touched my cheek. "You're a good boy, Taz, you really are, but you don't know shit. Kittery went to prison a few years ago. There ain't nothing left of his old life."

"What?"

"Burglary charge."

Burglary at nearly seventy years old is about drugs—stealing to buy a hit. Tomato Red and Lovey didn't fall apart for lack of crowds. Drugs killed them—drugs and Kittery's jealous theft of the tape.

"Junkies don't make it past seventy, Taz, he probably already went to Glory."

"No. Stones has him. Living at one of the clubs in Zachary City or something."

I watched an angry, deep red flood her face. Just as quickly it emptied until she was just resigned. "Nigel, hand me the bag, please."

Out of that cash bag came two thousand dollars. I tried to refuse but Dorothy is not a woman to be trifled with. "I can't buy your tapes but maybe this will help you and Cotton."

So I took the cash as she asked Nigel to play her slow mix. Otis Spann's "What Will Become of Me" poured through the house speakers and she gently pushed me to the drums. I hesitated, but she dug her fingers into my ribs to get me moving. Truthfully, I was nervous, maybe scared, but I let her push me, didn't I? I wanted to feel the drummer's throne beneath my ass, the pedals under my feet, a hard set of sticks in my hands.

Spann segued into Champion Jack Dupree's "Georgiana," and I was back onstage. This had been one of the duo's fav tunes and they played it everywhere. I fell into the music, lost myself like Daddy always did. But it opened an old, weathered crack in my heart, one I had believed—hoped—was healed. I'd gunned for the big show for years; different bands playing different music, one-night stands all over the country, but never got anywhere. Not even circuit-famous like Tomato Red and Lovey. Never banked good money, never cut a legit album, never had any endorsement deals. I'd never played sold-out houses or heard cheering masses.

Instead, I'd spent my entire musical life with what barmen called a "smattering of applause."

Two hours later, my hands blissfully tired, blisters painfully delicious, I left the barman a tip and told him to give my thanks to Dorothy. He said he enjoyed my playing and told me to stop by any time.

Then I hit Texas State Highway 22, headed west.

"Cal. Hey, it's Taz. How you doing, man?"

He was groggy. "The hell time is it?"

"Eleven, maybe? Sorry for calling so late, but I thought you'd be up…recording the next big thing. You always had a great ear."

A beat of silence, like stop time.

Then, "The hell you want?"

"Come on. Weren't we always friends?"

"Friends? You left me hold a pretty large bag, *friend*."

Total bullshit. Cal Tullo, president/producer/arranger/booking agent for Tullo Records in Waco, Texas, had been my first record offer. Nothing more than a scam. A week before recording was supposed to start, Cal hadn't signed a contract, hadn't set a schedule, hadn't hired any studio musicians, hadn't done any pre-production work. But had sent me a schedule of studio charges and an estimate of what I'd owe after recording was done.

Telling Cal to fuck off was one of the hardest things I'd ever done. Shoulda been easy—he was screwing me and doing it by playing on something I wanted desperately—but it wasn't. Part of me whispered, "He'll come through," even though I knew with bone-shattering certainty there would be no album.

So I went on a coke/booze/street pussy-fueled binge that lasted the better part of two weeks and landed me in jail twice.

"Calling about my first two albums. The masters are for sale. Wanted to talk to you first. The songs, the outtakes, the studio chatter, and...." I let the anticipation build. "Tomato Red."

He laughed immediately. "Forty-year old recordings of Tomato Red with some no-name band playing shitty originals and God-awful covers? Fuck off, ya' cheap-ass wanna-be. They ain't worth the tape used to record them. Know what else? It's pretty shitty to call me and try—"

I hung up and hammered the accelerator. A mile down the road, I cranked up the stereo: Stevie Ray Vaughn's Carnegie Hall live shot, loud enough to drown out my head.

'Round about midnight, I pulled into Hico, Texas, and parked at a tonk where Tomato Red and Lovey used to play. One of my bands had played here a few times, though I'd never seen a line of people like what I saw now. It snaked down the street and around the corner.

"Taz." Hubby's face lit up as he took money from a couple of couples and let them in. "The world's hottest drummer. Hotter than hell."

"Great album," I said. "Kiss's second."

Hubby laughed. "Early Kiss...when they were still worth a shit. Been awhile, hasn't it? God, it'd be great to hear you banging again."

"Thanks, Hubs, but all I do is lay it down." I mimed playing a drum set. "*Boom-ba cha-ta boom-ba cha-ta.* That's it."

The crowd was pushy to get in. The women were already dancing. Their boots clacked on the sidewalk, their jeans faded and tight, their shirts buttoned to just below breast line, while their dates wore equally tight Wranglers and hats that were totally broke-down over their eyes ala Toby Keith—a comfortable cliché in middle-class cowboy chic.

"Good crowd."

"Great band tonight. Hardcore outlaw. They're going somewhere. Like Waylon and Willie big. Hey, you should sit in. Two or three songs. Local celeb kind of thing."

God, how much I'd always wanted to play for a crowd this big and enthusiastic. "I'm not a local celeb, Hubby. Besides, I got something else going tonight. Does involve me playing, though, since that obviously gets your rocks off."

"Yeah?"

"Masters from *As The Crow Flies* and *Purple Cane Road.*"

"The first two records?"

"Deluxe production package. All the songs, all the outtakes, all the studio chatter. But I also have…." I paused. "Tomato Red."

"Really?"

"We cut five songs with him, but the producer didn't think they fit the vibe. I'm looking for a deal, so I came to you."

He laughed. "First, no doubt."

"Absolutely first. Well…close to first."

"Thanks for the blowjob but what's going on, Taz? I hear Tomato Red is dead. That's a damn shame. Really is. I loved having him play here. Made that damned steel guitar sing."

"Not dead but getting real close. Hubby, I need a deal."

"What's up?"

"Kittery. He's in Zach City, living in some old trailer at a joint he used to sing at."

Hubby laughed. "That old fart, the way I hear it, is flapping his gums about a comeback. Record and tour and whatever. Call it the 'Not Quite Folsom' Tour."

"And Johnny Cash spins in his grave."

"He ain't just somewhere in Zach City, Taz." Hubby licked his lips. "One of Stones's old whore trailers. At Gun Barrel. Ain't a club anymore, though. Just a shooting gallery, really. Kittery sucks down heroin and booze all day, the way I hear it." Knowledge flickered across Hubby's face. "Oh, shit. You want the tape Kittery stole. And Stones wants his money."

"Yeah."

"Shit, he played that good, didn't he?"

"What?"

"Stones played you. See, before Kittery went in, he had a ton of markers. All over the state. Money he borrowed, some he stole. About six months before he got outta prison, Stones started paying those debts."

"And then Kittery paroled to Stones's place."

"Yep."

Son of a bitch. Stones had known about Daddy's tape and put himself perfectly between me and Kittery.

"Kinda ironic...you selling your tapes to get Tomato Red's tape with that jazz guy."

"I need twenty, and my tapes won't even get me ten."

"I'm sorry, man, I don't think they will, no."

Inside, the house music stopped booming and the crowd already inside ripped out a ballsy cheer. The people in line pressed forward but Hubby moved them back. "All full, ladies and gentlemen. I'll get you in as fast as I can, I promise. This is only their second set, we got all kinds of music left."

A chorus of decently good-natured boos answered him, and I laughed. How many times before shows and between sets had I walked the streets, talking to people, trying to get them interested in the band or the new album. Hated doing it, but I'd had no other choice. It's the worst part of being a working musician, when the music became a chore rather than a love.

Seeing me seduced by the band, Hubs grinned and disappeared inside. The band was rocking a hard version of the Light Crust

Doughboys' "Pussy, Pussy, Pussy" before segueing into Paycheck's "I'm The Only Hell My Mama Ever Raised." The shower of music made my blood pound a hard four on the floor.

Hubby popped back out and led me inside. He sat me in an empty spot near the stage with a clear view of the band. They were young and having a great time. No pretension or affect, just four guys playing hard and the crowd going berserk.

My heart broke.

I'd had so many shitty nights awake trying to understand why my music had never amounted to anything—empty regrets, I guess. But hearing a riff played just so or tasting the heartache some singers could wrench out of their voices always made me believe in the very sanctity of music. That belief sometimes made me feel, for just a heartbeat, that I hadn't wasted my life playing music.

The band quieted, vamping through an instrumental middle eight bars. The lead singer, brown hair long and jeans tight, stepped to the mic. "We got a celebrity here tonight."

The crowd cheered.

"His daddy is one of the greatest steel guitar players in the history of country music and nobody beats the drums better...." A wink to the audience and a shrug toward his own drummer. "Not even my guy."

The crowd cheered again, not for me, but for the joke.

Hubby sidled up next to me. "Go on up. They're cool with it."

I hadn't expected to find this; a new version of the same dream and a crowd cheering with heat and passion and intensity I'd never heard. With my hesitation, the guy at the mic, guitar strapped low, waved me up.

"Get him up here," the singer howled.

My heart stopped; my breath dried in my throat. My hands tingled in spite of a storm of anxiety. They were good, these guys. I was in awe, but also scared to death.

The crowd got lusty but not for me. They had no idea who I was. They were cheering because the singer asked them to. They didn't give a crap who I was or whether or not I played, just so long as the music started again quick.

In the end, after a lifetime of those empty regrets, I slipped out the side door, hopped in the car, and headed for Zachary City.

Zachary City at four a.m.

I pulled to the side of the road and called.

"Yeah?" Voice was as heavy as the oil in the West Texas air.

"I've got his money."

"Yet you ain't at his door."

"Got no interest in getting shot and buried in his onion garden. I'm going to see Kittery. Stones wants his money, he'll be there. He'd better come alone, too, I don't want to kill any of his flunkies tonight."

I hung up and got to Gun Barrel quick. It was boarded over but with a few parking-lot lights still alive and tossing a weak white onto a cracked and broken lot. The place had never been much when my band played it, but now it was less than that.

On the lot's far edge was a trailer with a flat tire, taped-over windows, and steps that leaned sideways. A bonfire near it licked maybe three feet into the air. There was also a crappy aluminum lawn chair.

Which Kittery sat in.

Naked but for a single sock. Death-grip on a bottle of Calvert.

He offered me the bottle after he'd sucked a long pull. He nodded toward the dilapidated building. "Come for the show? Ain't singing tonight, maybe tomorrow night. Any night I want. Stones keeps the stage open for me. Getting back in shape, asshole. Already recorded eleven songs. Ol' Daddy got an album coming out?" He drank hard, took a weak, dribbly piss into the fire. "Fuck no, 'cause he wasn't shit without me."

"I want the tape."

Holding his flopper, he downed another swallow. "The tape. Fucking idiot. You know where I been?"

"Yeah, Kittery, you've been—"

"I been *down*, bitch, stacking hard time in a Texas prison so get the fuck outta—"

"I made a call, Kittery. You've been in Diboll stacking weaksister time with the other geriatric burnouts pushing walkers at the Duncan Unit. Fuck your hard time. *Daddy* stacked hard time when you stole his tape 'cause you were jealous he got to play with the musician he admired most in the entire world and that *wasn't you.*"

"Goddammit, my name is Lovey."

I dashed around the fire and shoved my gun against his head. He yelped and fell back into the aluminum chair.

"I hear you got my money."

Stones.

Kittery choked out a laugh. "How about it now, you little bitch."

I walked around the fire so I could see Stones clearly. I pointed my gun, but he didn't raise his hands. "What about *my* money?"

"Ain't that the shits? I thought this was about you paying me twenty thousand."

"No, it's about the eight-thousand-four-hundred-nineteen dollars you owe me off the tour."

His laugh boomed over the empty lot. "Ten years ago. Move on."

"Like you from your slots? Difference between you and me is I pay my debts."

"Speaking of…my money in your car?"

I fobbed the trunk open and motioned him toward it. "I won't shoot you in the back, asshole. When I kill you, it'll be face to face."

In the flickering orange of the flames, he smirked. The hair on the back of my neck tingled. I looked at his car—I hadn't even heard it drive up, I'd been so focused on Kittery—but saw nothing.

At the trunk, he laughed. "The fuck is this?"

"You've just gone into the record biz."

"Don't think so, pal. I do a cash-only business." I followed his gaze to his car but still saw no one.

"Those tapes are the masters of *As the Crow Flies* and *Purple Cane Road*."

"Yeah, you sold like fourteen copies," Stones said.

"'Cause Taz Niebank, a-k-fucking-a Mr. Memorial, ain't Tomato Red and Lovey," Kittery said.

"Kittery, shut your craphole," I said. To Stones, I said, "Those tapes include all the songs, all the outtakes and alternate versions, the studio chatter, and five previously unreleased songs featuring Tomato Red. Package it however you want, charge whatever you want. You'll make some coin. But label them as Tomato Red's band. His name will make you money and we'll be square."

After slamming my trunk closed, Stones came toward me. I saw his barely perceptible glance to his car and my nuts tightened. "Fuck those tapes. I'm not a record man. I run clubs to sell drugs for the boys down south, I sell booze and cigs with no tax stamps, I whore men and women, I hire coyotes over the border both directions for people, guns, drugs, cash—whatever I can sell. Does that sound like records?"

"It's just like you said, Stones." Kittery's voice was high. "He came for me."

I tried to keep Stones and his car both in my sight. "Came for the tape. That's all."

"Lovey, grab that ol' boy's tape."

My heart froze. At that moment, I didn't give shit one that Stones had played me, had buried Kittery in booze and smack to get me here. All that mattered, as Kittery came out of his trailer holding a couple Ampex tape boxes, were those tapes.

I got them, Daddy, I almost got them. I'll be home today.

Daddy had been in California, hired to record some country-pop bullshit, and Kessel had been next door, working on some album or another. When the day had been done, they stumbled across each other and started talking. They started playing and Barney's engineer had been smart enough to turn the machines on. Four hours later, Barney handed Daddy those tapes, shook his hand, and they parted company. As simple and pure as that.

"Why'd you lose your mind on my slots?"

I stepped forward until I was in his face. "Because I didn't have the balls to kill you."

When he chuckled, "Still don't," Kittery tossed the tapes onto the fire.

Anger exploded and I raised the .45. Stones's eyes flamed into a confidence that scared the crap outta me so I fired instantly; a bullet into his gut, harsh and painful. Before he hit the ground, I fired four times through the windshield of his car. Third shot caught someone rising from the backseat. The man's head disappeared, and his gun fell out the passenger window.

"Shitshit." Kittery howled like a shot mutt and fell backward over the aluminum chair.

I kicked my way through the fire, knocking the tapes out of the flames. The boxes were already burned and one of the tapes had melted into a brown goo, but the other was intact.

Daddy and Barney Kessel; everything that music meant to Daddy. Except—

The tape was a quarter-inch thick, dotted with white splice-tape.

I blinked, confused. Quarter-inch?

"You motherfucker." Stones tried to yell but pain and maybe surprise had taken most of his voice. "You shot me. Kittery, he killed me."

Quarter-inch tape? That wasn't right. They hadn't recorded on quarter-inch.

"One-inch tape, not quarter-inch." I leaned down toward Stones. "Where's the tape, motherfucker?"

Stones spit in my face. "Stupid shit. Ain't no tape."

Kittery shook his head, scared to death. "No tape, Taz. Sorry, sorry. No tape. Sold it long time ago 'cause I needed the bread, man."

I shot Kittery, too. Probably shouldn't have but his jealous theft of that tape from Daddy started this shitshow so what the hell did I care? Daddy was dying, my two heart attacks said I probably didn't have long for this world, either, and the tape was gone.

Fuck both of them.

I searched Kittery's trailer just in case but found squat, so I left quick. When the sun cracked the horizon over Zach City, I was already out of town. Found an abandoned oil-pumpjack station miles down the highway and parked.

And cried for two hours.

Before I got home, I stopped in Marshall. Stones's goons were at a by-the-hour flop, exactly where a few calls had told me they probably would be. I knocked until someone answered and I killed them, too. "Fucking shoot up Daddy's guitar?" Then I pissed on both of them.

When I made it to Uncertain, I found Daddy playing. A jarring song, words from different tunes, the key of his steel guitar something different than what he sang. But he played with a joyous rapture. He stopped when he saw me. "Taz! You're home, boy."

"I am, Daddy."

His face went tight. "Did he have it?"

I swallowed. I'd thought about this moment all the way home. "Yeah, Daddy, he did."

The man, so close to the end of the show it broke my heart, hugged me. What had been a bear hug years ago was now a whisper from a nighttime breeze. "Oh, thank you, Taz, I knew I could count on you."

"Well, Daddy...see...the thing is, he had to move recently. Lost his lease or something, I don't know. So everything of his is packed up in a storage unit."

"What?"

"He's got the tape and he's going to find it as soon as he gets home from his daughter's house. She was sick, see, but as soon as he gets home, he'll find it and send it. I gave him our address so don't worry. We'll get it in a few days. Maybe a week."

Relief poured over him. He shook my hand and started singing again.

From near his chair, as broken as he was, I grabbed his flashlight and played it across him, a spotlight from one of the old clubs, while he sang and picked random notes on his guitar.

"I love you, Daddy."

"Love you, too, boy. How 'bout 'Whiskey River'?"

"Yeah, that's a good one."

ORCHIDS AND CHITLIN GREASE

Kimberly B. Richardson

She lived her life in black and white. Stark contrasts with a cup of tea always in her hand. She wore her signature scent in the hopes that someone would walk by, smell her perfume, and think, "That woman needs to be in a novel." She searched for jazz vinyl in vintage stores and later listened to them while eating croissants. She knew of something more than the punch clock and desperately prayed that it wasn't some cruel joke. She worshiped Audrey Hepburn and created a shrine in her name that consisted of an empty bottle of Chanel No. 5, dead roses, and a well-read copy of Breakfast at Tiffany's. *She made love with her eyes while her purple-stained lips remained frozen in a hushed smile. She adored it when someone touched her skin to make contact with her soul. She dreamt of becoming a muse for a poverty-stricken artist who couldn't bear to touch her for fear of shattering their illusion.*

"Welcome," she told me one night, "to why I deliberately smear my makeup with tears. Why I watch French films on mute. Why I can't get up from the bed without a kiss. Why I love old books. And why I love you more than I should."

* * *

Jake stared at his notebook as the last word settled onto the paper. *Love me more than she should,* he thought with a grimace as he finished off his second shot of cheap whiskey.

The bartender was quick to fill the glass with more of the brown liquor and without conversation. The surly older black man had seen all kinds of people—those who wanted to talk your damn ear off as soon as they set foot inside the joint; those who came only for the sake of "doing something Southern" and risky; and those, like Jake, who just wanted to be left alone so they could get stinking drunk. *And,* thought the bartender, *he's doin' a good job of it.*

Jake reached for his crumpled pack of cigarettes and shook one out without his eyes ever leaving his notebook. He stuck the cig in his mouth and slowly lit it with his trusty lighter. The smoke caused his eyes to water, yet his gaze never left what he had written.

"She must have taken your dog or something," said a voice nearby. The voice didn't register with Jake until he felt a hand slowly touch his arm. He looked down at his arm, then the hand touching him, and then finally at the woman who owned the hand. Jake stared at her in silence as the woman stared right back. "So, what kind of dog was it?"

Jake blinked once, then muttered, "I'm not some damn country music song."

The woman pulled her hand back and instead offered him a red-lipstick smile.

"Never said you were," she replied as she lit a black cigarette captured between her lips. "But whoever she was, you must have really been in love with her."

Jake snorted. The bartender refilled his shot glass, and he downed the entire shot.

The woman took a drag and then turned her gaze toward the band setting up in the corner. Chitlin Grease was the name of the blues band—the best in the area, she'd been told by a gas station attendant last night. The band consisted of a young black man on drums; a skinny, pasty white guitarist with long black hair dressed in a snakeskin suit who had a harmonica strapped around his mouth; and a curvy black woman with milk-chocolate skin who wore a tight red dress. Although the bar was half full, all eyes were on the band. They knew what to expect. The drummer tapped his drumsticks three times, and then the woman began to sing in a low and sultry tone:

Where were you the other day, baby?
Where were you the other day, baby?
I got tired of waiting by the phone
I guess you done run away...

The woman at the bar began to nod her head to the rhythm as others did too. Even the bartender grinned and began to shimmy behind the bar. The only person who wasn't taken by the music was Jake. He picked up his pencil, made a move as if to write more in his notebook, then set the pencil down and instead reached for his whiskey.

I'm feeling cold without you, baby
I'm feeling cold
I'm feeling cold without you, baby
The sun don't shine no mo'

Jake finally turned around to face the band, mostly because the bartender refused to give him more whiskey until the band took a break. He sipped on his latest shot, trying to make it last, as the band played on in the corner. He didn't want any music, didn't want any kind of sound except the sound of him drinking and the sound of the whiskey being poured into the glass. He glanced at the woman who had spoken with him and finally got a look at her. She wore her black hair pulled back into a thick ponytail, showing off her slender ears. Her only makeup was the lipstick. *Women like her don't need makeup,* he thought.

Natural beauty. Silver hoop earrings in her ears. A black top with jeans that seemed to hug her curvy body. Black boots that looked as though she could kick someone's ass with a smile and no regrets. She crushed out her cigarette as she moved even more to the music. He refocused on the band and, after a while, found himself nodding along with the music. *That lead singer had a set of pipes in her,* he thought as he sipped on his shot again.

After three songs and much applause, the guitarist said, "All right, we are Chitlin Grease, for those of you who don't know!" The audience laughed. "I'm Snake Oil, the drummer is Flash, and our singing angel is Miss Ivone!" The applause grew louder as Miss Ivone took a florid bow. Even Jake clapped. "Folks, we gotta take a break to get some drinks in us, but we will be right back! Tip the bartender well, 'cause he gotta take care of that wooden leg!"

Some of the people in the bar laughed as the low sounds of conversation now took over. Jake and the woman turned back around to face the bartender, who held a bottle of whiskey with both hands. He made a motion to pour into Jake's glass; Jake held a hand over it and shook his head.

The bartender then moved to the woman, and she said, "One ice cube with it."

While the bartender fixed her drink, she lit another black cigarette and took a deep drag from it. As she blew out smoke, Jake wondered if he smelled lavender coming from it.

"Are you smoking potpourri or something?" he asked, trying to make a modicum of conversation with her. Not that he cared. The woman turned to face him again and took another drag, then blew the smoke right into his face. Jake didn't even cough.

"I picked up this bad habit while in Paris," she said as she waved the smoke away with slender and quite long hands. "Of course, it's not easy to be a writer and photographer and *not* smoke if you live in Paris. The name is Vivien Tea." She held out her hand, and Jake noticed that her fingernails were deep purple.

"Jake," he said. He took her hand and gave it a good shake.

"Jake Swank."

Vivien crinkled her nose. "Swank? Seriously?"

"It's my pen name," Jake replied. "Only my mom knows my real name. My fans know my pen name. It's easier that way."

Vivien shrugged. "Then Jake Swank it is. What do you write?"

"Underground pieces, the kind for those who proclaim that Kerouac was a god. Got about ten books out now."

Vivien smirked. "And I'm assuming that I can get your books on Amazon?"

Jake snorted as he finished his shot and then lit up a cigarette. "Look, I'm just trying to be nice and all, considering we're both siting in a juke joint called The Black Sole and listening to a band named Chitlin Grease." Jake turned away from her, set his cigarette in the ashtray, and picked up his pencil once more.

"And again, I say to you—she must have taken your dog," Vivien replied. She took another long draw from her black cigarette.

Jake seemed to ignore her as he furiously wrote in his notebook, only to close it a moment later and set the pencil on top.

"Yeah, I'm the classic 'down on his luck' guy," Jake replied. He picked up his cigarette and took a deep drag. "I saw her, she saw me, we fell in love, she dumped me, I never got over it, and decided to travel. There," he said. He crushed out his cigarette in the ashtray then slowly clapped. "Now you know. And no, there was no dog involved. More like a...goldfish."

Vivien's eyes widened. She tried not to laugh, yet the laugh came out anyway. "A goldfish?" she cried. "Seems like you do have a heart."

"I loved Hush Puppy," Jake replied with a grimace, only to have it replaced with a smile. "Best attack goldfish we ever had."

The bartender handed Vivien her drink and she downed it in one gulp, then cracked the ice cube in her mouth.

"Damn, girl," said Jake, "you've got a set of choppers."

"I learned from the best," Vivien replied after swallowing the ice pieces. "I, too, got dumped. His name was Adrian. Claimed

145

he loved me and wanted us to make the writing world tremble at our feet. Only problem was that he enjoyed having a woman named Simone tremble under him, if you know what I mean." Vivien winked and the bartender poured her another shot, followed by two ice cubes.

Jake wanted to read his piece to Vivien; he knew that a stranger hearing his latest words would somehow validate him. Just as he was about to ask her, the band returned to the stage to much applause and whistles. Jake and Vivien returned their attention to the band.

"All right, folks," said Snake Oil as the other members got into their places, "here we go!" He started off with a riff on his harmonica, signaling Miss Ivone to sing—

I'm a wrecking machine of a woman
And don't you forget it
I'm a wrecking machine of a woman
And don't you forget it
'Cause if you try to run me over
This woman ain't gonna forget it

Jake wondered if Lucy would have ever joined him at this place. She probably thought that it wasn't underground enough for her. He sighed; some days, it was good to have her out of his life. Others, not so much. This night...

He glanced at Vivien when she lit up another cigarette. No attraction at all, yet she was probably the most confident woman he'd ever met. *Of all places to meet such a woman,* he thought with a chuckle. He also had another thought: *no more whiskey.* He glanced at his glass and something clicked inside him. Just no more. He'd spent too many days and nights lost in a fog of booze and that itch for the edge in whatever form it took.

He used to want to feel the rush of life and did whatever it took to find it. Then, Lucy appeared during an art gallery exhibit. He wore his usual jeans and tight black shirt, mingled with the look of nonchalance. As he stared at a framed painting of raggedy jeans while barely listening to the artist talking about how art was found everywhere, he glanced to his left and saw Lucy. Lucy, the woman with the spiky red hair and fitted three-piece masculine suit. His heart literally melted. He struck up a conversation with her, she suggested they do dinner down the street, and by the end of the month they were in love. She encouraged him and his passion for writing and he encouraged her and her music. After three months passed, he asked her to move in with him. That's when all hell broke loose. She went from his main cheerleader to someone who couldn't even stand the way he typed. She claimed that he never supported her and her search for pure music. Whenever he tried to give into whatever demands she made, she claimed that he was really doing the opposite. She wanted someone who would fight with and against her, changing viewpoints at the drop of a hat. Jake suddenly found himself enjoying the comforts of a bottle, and soon Lucy dumped him while they were at a concert in Boston. He returned to their home before she did (she wanted to enjoy Boston more by herself), gathered up all of her things, and then set them on fire while he made s'mores and listened to The Clash.

Vivien, although completely engrossed in the music, was thinking about Jake. He seemed like a dime a dozen—the type who claimed he understood the soul in a rough and harsh manner. She ate men like him for breakfast. And yet, he did have a pet goldfish named Hush Puppy. Country song be damned.

The night continued as Chitlin Grease played on, much to the adoration of their fans. More people entered the bar after the band started their second set, making Vivien wonder just how popular this band truly was. Did they have any albums? Why hadn't she heard of them before? She thought about Adrian and how he would have loved this kind of place. As much as she was fascinated with the French, Adrian was completely *gaga* over Americans. He seemed to think they could do no wrong. They used to stay up late sometimes, debating how Americans handled things versus the French. She always thought that the French handled matters with style and grace. Adrian felt that Americans handled matters with no nonsense and elbow grease (a term he still couldn't figure out but loved how it sounded).

When she first arrived in France, she was wide-eyed yet not naive. When she chose to become a writer and photographer, she wanted to experience it all. And she did. From parties at lavish mansions, filled to the brim with beautiful people, money, and lots of drugs, to concerts in sewers with Goth bands that screamed of death and rose petals. She traveled all over the world in an attempt to capture the essence of what made humans so damned human. And she found the answer—it didn't matter. By the time she reached this small town only two nights ago and checked into the only hotel, she was on the verge of experiencing burnout. She wanted to return home to New Orleans and just fade into the wallpaper, yet she knew that once she attempted such a thing, she would be packing her bags for yet another "assignment."

I'm alone and so are you
I'm alone, baby, and so are you
By the time we ever come together
There'll be no more two

After a while, Miss Ivone made a motion to the musicians, then said, "All right, folks. Time for a slow one. Grab someone you love and feel the music." Immediately, people jumped up with partners and made their way to the dance floor.

"We don't love each other," Jake said with a grin, "but do you wanna dance?"

Vivien lifted her hand for him, and the two made their way to the dance floor.

Jake gently wrapped an arm around her.

"I won't break," Vivien said with a soft laugh as she wrapped her arms around him. The music began, slow and sweet, and couples found the groove and moved along with it. Miss Ivone's voice carried throughout the place. She sang of love and pecan pie, of holding your baby close and never letting go.

Jake scanned the place with lazy eyes while trying not to think about Vivien's perfume. Lavender mingled with lemon? Lime? Was it aftershave? He chuckled, causing Vivien to pull away with a questioning look.

"Did I stumble?" she asked.

"No, it's just that...damn." Jake glanced away for a moment, then back at her face. "What is that, lavender and lime?"

"Oh."

Jake detected a bit of blush on her cheeks.

"Lime and lavender. Good nose."

"It's my job."

Vivien grinned and leaned back into him. The song carried on as the couples twirled each other around. Jake and Vivien continued their tight embrace, each fearing that the other would let go. For some reason, they both needed to feel the other person, needed to know that they were not alone. As Miss Ivone ended the song on a low note, the couples and those seated gave her a round of applause. Vivien and Jake pulled apart and added to the applause, then reclaimed their seats at the bar. The bartender held two freshly filled glasses of whiskey and handed them over.

Jake held up a hand. "Thanks, my man, but I'm done for the night. And probably a long time after that." He lit up a cigarette and blew out two perfect circles.

"Are you staying in town tonight?" Vivien asked him.

Jake raised an eyebrow. "Why?"

Vivien shrugged her shoulders. "Wanna go for a walk? Nothing more, believe me."

Jake stared into her face for a full ten seconds, then nodded.

"Check out the Hand Cemetery down the street," the bartender said in a gravelly voice. Then he downed both glasses of whiskey.

149

"It never closes. Good lighting. Perfect for two wandering souls." Vivien gave him a salute and then slid off her stool, while Jake grabbed his bag. Vivien slung her bag over her shoulder, and the two made their way out of the bar just as Miss Ivone began a rowdy song about how her man was "well hung."

The town consisted of several houses, the inn, the juke joint, a small library (much to their surprise), several stores, and a cemetery located right in the middle. As the two walked along, the sounds of the night greeted them: a woman yelling at a man for having lipstick on his collar; a dog howling at the moon; some kids playing in front of a house; and two old women seated on the front porch of another, laughing about some distant memory that still seemed fresh to them.

"I'd never even heard of this town until a friend of mine told me about Chitlin Grease," Jake said. "They were really good, though."

"Yeah, they were," Vivien replied as her mind was half with him and half back in Paris. "I kinda hate to leave the place, ya know?"

Jake nodded.

"This is what makes the South *the* South, aside from the food, the literature, the art, the..." She let her voice trail off as she noticed Jake looking at the houses. She asked, "What's on your mind?"

"People who live in small towns tend to have better lives than us city folk," he mused aloud. "Maybe I'm seeing them through burned-out, rose-colored glasses, but yeah." They reached and walked through the fancy iron gate. Light posts were positioned here and there throughout the small, well-maintained cemetery.

"Believe in ghosts?" Vivien joked as she lit a cigarette.

"Not really, but then again, New York is too loud for ghosts. If anything, they probably gentrified themselves."

Vivien took a deep drag from her cigarette, exhaled, and then began to cackle. "Gentrified ghosts?" she said while laughing. "That sounds like a really good story plot."

Jake grinned as he, too, lit a cigarette. He then slowly walked around the area, making sure to look at all of the tombstones. *Each one of these pieces of rock is all we have left of these people,* he thought. He glanced over to find Vivien wandering through the other side. He stopped in front of a stone: *Paula Pass, Born 1919–Died 1969. Well Loved Librarian. The Words Will Never Stop.* Jake crouched and took his notebook from his bag. He wrote down the inscription with a pencil, then stood up and walked to the next one. *Each one of them has a history,* he thought, just as Vivien walked up to him.

"I just found a man named Lucien Orchid," she said with a grin. "Apparently, he was an author from here who traveled all over the world and returned here to die."

"How Southern Gothic," Jake replied. He ran a hand through his hair.

"I'm sure the library has a couple of his books," she said as she cast her gaze toward the building. "I'm going back to look at some more. Found anyone interesting?"

"So far, a librarian named Paula Pass. You're right; I think that library will have a lot to offer us."

Vivien raised an eyebrow. "Us?"

Jake raised his hands in defense. "Not like that, but come on...can you feel something here? Anything?"

Vivien raised her face to the night sky as several breezes played with her hair.

"Maybe we've located another Crossroads."

Vivien snorted. "If that's the case, then I'm conducting an interview with the Devil."

Jake grinned, then resumed his search.

After they wandered through the cemetery for an hour, neither was ready to go to their room. Instead, they returned to the Black Sole for more music.

"If anything, we can listen to more good music, then stumble into our beds with books covering our faces," Jake said, making Vivien cackle again. When they walked back into the juke joint, they found the place completely packed with people, all of whom were drenched in sweat and cigarette smoke.

"Seems the regulars finally showed up," Vivien yelled as Jake led the way to the bar.

The bartender's eyes went wide, then narrowed as he poured whiskey for them. Jake handed his glass to the bartender and requested water. After the bartender looked at him like he'd suddenly grown horns, he gave Jake his order. When Jake received his glass, both raised them in salute, along with the bartender, and downed them without a second thought.

Jake slowly opened one eye, followed by the other, while a jackhammer pounded in his head. He groaned as he sat up and reached for his cigarettes. Seconds later, he stood outside in his pajamas, trying to enjoy the first cigarette of the day.

"Damn, man," Jake groaned as he lowered his head to the railing. "What the hell? Stupid rotgut. I didn't even have that much." He grinned in spite of the pain it caused. He slowly raised his head, took another drag from his cigarette, and noticed Vivien leaning against the railing some down the way. She wore black pajamas and was enjoying her first black cigarette of the day. He raised a hand in greeting, causing her to walk toward him. Even though her hair looked a little bed-messy, she looked just as fresh as ever.

"Did you shower or something?" he said. He threw his cigarette to the ground. "You look perfect."

"Ah, well, I learned my drinking skills from French guys," Vivien replied. She blew smoke in his face, causing him to cough. "Slow and steady. So," she said as she threw her cigarette to the ground, "when did you want to go to the library? They open at nine."

"I was being serious about that." He started feeling a little better.

"So was I. Can't stay long, though. You up for some research?"

Jake grinned. "I hope the cafe's got good black coffee."

The Over Cafe did, actually. So much so that Jake had three cups along with his shortstack pancakes and bacon. Vivien had scrambled eggs and toast with tea, which she always carried with her, and a waitress named Abigail was more than happy to give her hot water. When the two finished their breakfast, they made their way to the library and were surprised to find that it was well stocked and consisted of two floors, along with a basement that held their bookstore. They strolled up to the front desk; Jake asked about Paula Pass, while Vivien asked about Mr. Orchid.

"Oh, he was quite the gentleman," said the elderly librarian assisting Vivien. Jake had already left the desk with a list of books to locate. "He was quite the talk of the town around here. Always dressed so nicely and used to give us girls fresh orchids when we were younger. He wanted to share the beauty of the world with us. He wrote so many books over the course of his life; we all wondered when he had the time!"

"I bet," Vivien said with a dazzling smile.

"However," the librarian said as she leaned closer and her smile faded away, "there were rumors that. . ." She trailed off as she glanced around and then whispered, "Mr. Orchid left this world too soon."

Vivien blinked several times in confusion. "Left too soon?"

The librarian took a deep breath, exhaled, and then replied, "Murdered." Vivien gasped as a hand flew up to her mouth. "But, it's just a rumor," the librarian quickly added in a harsh whisper while waving her hands in an attempt to calm Vivien down. "Don't say anything," she added in a rush. "Please, girl, don't say anything, you hear?"

"I don't know anyone here," Vivien offered, "so who would I tell?" Yet deep down, she knew she had to tell Jake. He was an outsider. He was safe. Vivien nodded her thanks and then left the desk to find Jake. When she finally found him thumbing through several books while seated at one of the study tables, her heart was racing. She plopped down in a chair next to him.

"Jake," she whispered, startling him out of his research. His eyes went wild, only to soften when he saw that it was Vivien.

"Find anything interesting on Mr. Orchid?" he asked with a laugh, only to fall silent when he noticed her grave expression.

"He was murdered," Vivien mouthed the words barely above a whisper. "Mr. Orchid. Murdered," Jake glanced away for a moment and then ran his hands through his hair. He exhaled a steady breath.

"How do you know?"

"The librarian told me," she replied. "She claimed it was a rumor but . . . I don't know." She leaned back in her chair. Jake stroked his chin while deep in thought. "Don't they have a saying down here to let the dead stay dead?" Jake continued to stroke his chin in silence.

"I've got an idea," Jake slowly replied.

Later that evening, the two found themselves back at the Black Sole.

"Look," Jake said as the bartender handed shots of whiskey to them, "I know it's crazy—"

"Damn right it is," Vivien interjected with a quick nod to the bartender.

"Still," Jake said as he held up his hands in mock surrender, "I think it will work."

"This is known as writer suicide, ya know."

Jake shot his whiskey and enjoyed the quick burn down his

throat. Ever since they left the library, Jake's mind buzzed with his plan. Yes, it was stupid. Yes, it meant taking a chance. However, what if? What if he didn't do it? Would it make a difference at all? "It may be suicide for you," Jake finally replied, "but to me, it's the chance I've been waiting for."

Vivien downed her shot as well, wiped her mouth with the back of her hand, and said as she lit a cigarette, "Then I can't wait to hear about your discoveries. From my home. Far away from here." She glanced at her hands and then returned her gaze to his face as a smile appeared on her lips. "It's a risk but why not. That's been your entire life anyway, right? By the way, what did you find out about Miss Paula? Anything like what I discovered?"

"Nothing really," Jake replied, only to halt when he felt the eyes of the bartender on him. He slowly turned in his chair to face the quiet man.

"She was one of the best people in the area," the bartender said in a soft tone. "Taught me how to read when no one else cared. She was a good woman who died loved by everyone but the man who deflowered her."

"I bet. Hey," Jake asked with a sly grin as he leaned forward, "know anything about Mr. Lucian Orchid?"

The bartender leaned back and folded his arms over his chest. "Why?" His voice sounded like pitch-black gravel. Jake wondered if perhaps he had overstepped his boundaries. The bartender remained still for five long seconds, then reached down behind the bar. When he stood back up, he had a small blue cloth book in his hand. He slid the book toward Jake and Vivien and then wandered off to assist another customer. Jake opened the book to reveal a small photo wedged between the pages. Vivien took the photo, stared at it, and then handed it to Jake.

"You do realize that I'm now helping you?" Vivien said as she remembered she had another shot of whiskey. She quickly downed it, took another drag from her cigarette, and sighed. Jake stared at the photo, almost willing it to speak to him. Yet, the image it conveyed was enough—a well-dressed black man, face down on the ground with several knife wounds in his back. Just then, the bartender returned, glanced at them, and then poured more whiskey for them. Vivien pushed hers to the side.

"Why?" Jake asked the bartender in a low tone as he placed the photo back into the book. "Why show this to me?"

"Because you asked," the bartender replied as he took the book. "Lots of blind and deaf people here." He shrugged. "Lots of people wanna stay that way, too." He walked off again, leaving the two to ponder his grave words.

"Well, what do you think? A well-known author from a Southern town returns home, gets murdered, and no one wants to talk about it? Call me crazy, but I want to know what really happened. And . . . I know you do, too," Jake said as the band started up their performance for the evening.

"I think this is a rabbit hole I want to go down," Vivien yelled as she put out her cigarette and reached for her other shot of whiskey. "Should we toast to Mr. Orchid, as morbid as that sounds?" Jake took his glass and clinked it against hers.

An hour later, the bartender sat in a small room in the back of the bar. He closed his eyes and allowed the sounds of Chitlin Grease to take over his mind. Yet, he knew that it was impossible after talking to Jake and Vivien. He had explained that Mr. Lucian Orchid had given too many orchids to too many girls and that librarian Paula Pass had written the last page of Orchid's life.

He pulled the book from his pocket and opened it to the photo. He stared long and hard at it, hoping that Jake and Vivien had learned not to take their new love lightly, and then he closed the book again.

IF YOU'VE GOT
THE MONEY, HONEY

Michael Bracken

Moments after I awoke from a blackout drunk, two cowboys the size of Brahman bulls burst through the door of my motel room and the ugly one shoved the barrel of a snub-nosed .38 into my left nostril. "Where is she?"

I didn't need to ask who he meant because I'd only been with one woman since arriving in Chicken Junction, Texas: Crystal Dahl, a natural blond wearing a wedding ring as tight as her morals were loose.

I'd rolled into town with Buster Brown and His Big Hat Band the previous afternoon for a Saturday night gig at the Dew Drop Inn, a honky-tonk next door to the Dixie Motel where the two cowboys found me. I'd been a last-minute addition, joining the band just before leaving Nashville for their barnstorming South-western tour, hitting honky-tonks and dancehalls and county fairs throughout Oklahoma, Texas, New Mexico, and Arizona. I played rhythm guitar, sang harmony, and drank my earnings in a failed effort to forget what had driven me onto the road after having had steady employment as a studio musician performing on recordings by some of country and western's biggest names.

During the band's first break the previous evening, a wide-hipped waitress had brought me a beer. When I asked who sent it, she pointed to a big-haired blonde sitting alone at a tall two-top in the corner. My benefactor wore a white blouse, buttons straining to constrain her bullet bra, and a knee-length blue skirt with a single petticoat beneath. Low-heeled white cowboy boots completed her outfit, revealing a brief length of smooth shin between the scallop of her boots and the hem of her skirt. I lifted the beer bottle and tipped it slightly toward her in silent thanks. She also held a beer, and she tipped hers in return.

I knew I looked good. Like the rest of the band, I wore a western-style jacket—black with red roses embroidered near the shoulders—over a white shirt and black string tie, black slacks, and black cowboy boots. My dark hair was oiled back, and I was clean-shaven. Only Buster Brown wore a cowboy hat—an oversized ten-gallon Stetson—but he was compensating for his short stature. The hat was a gimmick conceived by the same manager who named Buster's band and sent him on the road in support of a single that had barely cracked the top hundred on the Billboard Country & Western Chart.

During the band's second set, I kept an eye on the blonde. She kept her right leg crossed over her left, and she bounced her foot in time with the music. Despite her sitting alone, none of the single men approached her, so during the second break I stepped off the stage and headed her direction. As I made my way through the tables, the wide-hipped waitress delivered two open beer bottles to the blonde's table and winked at me as she headed back to the bar.

Before I could speak, the blonde took my left hand in both of hers and said, "I've been watching your fingers. I like the way you use them."

Only then did I notice her wedding ring, a simple gold band a size too small for the slender finger it encircled. I had sworn off married women, but the way the blonde massaged my hand made me rethink my priorities. Instead of walking away, I sat.

Buster had introduced the band at the end of the first set, so I felt certain the blonde knew my name. I didn't know hers, though, so I asked.

"Dahl," she said. "Crystal Dahl."

"I'm pleased to meet you, Mrs. Dahl," I said.

She ran one fingernail across my palm, sending a shiver up my arm. "There's no reason to be so formal, Ernie. Call me Crystal."

The wide-hipped waitress brought one beer after another during the rest of that break, and during the next break we graduated from beer to whiskey shots. By the end of the show my playing had grown sloppy. The audience didn't notice, but Buster did. After the last song, he grabbed my arm and pulled me aside.

"I warned you, Ernie," he said. "I'm not warning you again."

I didn't pay much attention to what he said because I had a blonde who needed my attention. "Yeah, yeah," I told him. "I hear you. I got it."

After Buster walked off in disgust, I snagged a bottle of whiskey and put my Martin D-28 in its case, which Crystal offered to carry. So, with a whiskey bottle in one hand and my other arm wrapped around her, we crossed the parking lot to the Dixie Motel.

Once inside my room, Crystal was as eager to remove her clothes and show me her assets as I was to see them, and we fell onto the bed in a tangle of limbs before I demonstrated exactly what I could do with my fingers until I finally passed out.

I looked past the two cowboys. My guitar lay naked on the dresser, the case as gone as the Dahl who'd shared my bed. I pushed myself off the mattress, stepped to the window, and used a finger to open a gap in the blinds. The twelve-room Dixie Motel, recently built next to the Dew Drop Inn on the outskirts of town, had been the band's lodging. We had filled six of the twelve rooms, a luxury we didn't often enjoy while touring. More often than not we slept on the bus while traveling from show to show, and when we did have luxury accommodations, the band often crowded into a room with the bus driver while Buster Brown roomed by himself.

Save for a wood-paneled station wagon, the parking lot was empty.

"Where's Buster Brown?" I asked as I turned back to the cowboys. "Where's the band?"

"They blew town this morning."

Buster hadn't been kidding when he'd chewed me out the previous night.

I asked, "So, why are you here?"

"Someone cleaned out the safe over at the Dew Drop," the ugly one said. His name was Lucky, but with his face I didn't see how he could be. "Only two people knew the combination, and one of them is sitting over there with his thumb up his ass."

"He sent you over here to talk to me?"

"No," Lucky said. "Grover Dahl sent us. That was his wife you were seen leaving with last night. She ain't come home."

"Well, she isn't here."

"Put on some clothes," he said, "and you can tell him your own self."

The two cowboys escorted me across the parking lot, past a trio of pickup trucks and a two-seat Ford Thunderbird convertible with its top up, and into the Dew Drop Inn. Daylight did not become the place, and the smell did little for my queasy stomach. The honky-tonk had been a small Hudson dealership that went bust several years earlier, and the new owner had put in a bar, a stage in what once been the service bay, a small dance floor delineated by a rectangle of concrete painted red, and too many tables with mismatched chairs. The walls were covered with metal signs and dead animals and autographed photographs of touring acts that had passed through, none of them famous.

Two men were waiting in the office when the cowboys pushed me through the door. I recognized Elroy, the wiry little man sitting in front of the open safe, as the owner, and I figured the man in the wheelchair was Grover Dahl.

He was. Without preamble, he said, "My wife didn't come home this morning, and her car's still out there."

I looked at the stumps of his legs, one ending above the left knee, the other below the right knee.

He saw where I was staring and said, "I left them at Inchon."

Korea. He'd been there. I hadn't.

"I don't begrudge my wife her little flings with every guitar player who blows through town," he continued, "but she always comes home. This morning she didn't. So, where is she?"

"You find her," I said, "you tell her I want my guitar case back."

He glanced toward the open safe and then asked Elroy, "How much was in there?"

"Almost fifteen thousand," the honky-tonk owner said.

My eyes widened in surprise.

"The entire weekend take," he said, "and the other."

"A girl can go a long way with fifteen thousand dollars," I said.

Grover Dahl returned his attention to me. "If you had it, you wouldn't still be here," he said. His eyes narrowed. "Why *are* you still here? Shouldn't you have gone with the band?"

"They left me."

He considered a moment. "Opened up a seat, didn't it?"

"Yeah."

Grover called to the two cowboys waiting outside the office and told them to find Buster Brown and His Big Hat Band. He turned to me. "Where were they headed next?"

I shrugged. "West."

After the two cowboys left, Grover dismissed me, and I returned to the Dixie Motel. I showered, finished the last swallow of whiskey from the night before, and tallied my assets. I had my guitar and a suitcase full of clothes. I had not been paid for the previous night and had only seven dollars and eighty-two cents. I walked to the motel office to see how much another night would cost and discovered that Buster Brown had paid for my room through Wednesday morning.

I had nowhere to go and nothing to do once I got there, so I hung around town. Music was all I knew, so I finally returned to the honky-tonk to talk to Elroy. He gave me a job cleaning the place after hours and let me play for tips on Tuesday and Wednesday nights. I earned enough to rent two rooms with a bath and spent my off hours practicing songs I knew and teaching myself the popular tunes playing on country and western AM radio stations.

For the next few months I tried to hook up with every touring act that passed through the Dew Drop Inn, but none would have me. Those who hadn't heard about my reason for leaving Nashville knew why Buster Brown dumped me. Neither served as a stunning recommendation.

Before long, I began making time with Jolene, the wide-hipped waitress who had winked at me the first night. Auburn-haired and full-bodied, she was nothing like the big-haired blondes who usually caught my eye, but she was ready, willing, and able, and in a town where I knew no one else, that was more than enough for me.

One Wednesday, long after last call, I pushed open the office door and hesitated when Grover Dahl looked up from the stack of twenties he'd been counting. He sat behind the desk, so I couldn't see the stumps of his legs nor where his right hand went when he dropped it into his lap.

"Sorry," I said. "I didn't realize you were still here."

"Come in," he said. "Close the door."

I did as instructed, leaned my broom against the wall, and waited.

"Still haven't found my wife."

"That's what I heard."

"She say anything to you that night about leaving?"

What she'd said to me I wasn't about to repeat to her husband, but I'd done my best to give her what she'd asked for.

"Was she good?"

"Good?"

"Was my wife good in bed?"

"I—" The last man who had asked me that question—a successful record producer with an insatiable wife—had threatened to break my knuckles with a ball-peen hammer if I didn't leave Nashville. So, I'd signed on with Buster Brown and His Big Hat Band and wound up mopping floors and scrubbing toilets in the butt crack of Texas.

"She was a wildcat when we were younger," Grover continued, "but that's something else I lost at Inchon. I've been unable to satisfy her since I returned."

Hesitantly, I said, "Yeah. She was good, best I remember. I was drunk."

Grover narrowed his eyes.

"I can come back later," I said, "clean the office after you finish."

He didn't act as if he'd heard me. He pointed to the money covering the desk. "You know what this is?"

I shook my head.

"Redemption," he said. He lifted his hand from his lap and it held the snub-nosed .38 I'd had pressed into my left nostril several weeks earlier. "I don't figure you for the kind of joe that takes something that ain't yours—"

"Your wife."

I'd been too quick on the quip, but Grover smiled sadly. "You didn't take her," he said. "She gave herself to you—to you and to every other touring guitar player who would have her."

He'd made certain I knew I was nothing special, but I'd already figured that out.

He waved the .38 toward the door. "Go on," he said. "Clock out. I'll tell Elroy I let you go early."

* * *

Jolene lived in a mobile home parked at Riverview Estates—a place with no river and no view—and she answered my four-a.m. knock on her door. She'd showered and washed away the stench of cigarettes and alcohol that clung to us after a night at the Dew Drop Inn, and she wore an oversized blue robe. Without makeup and with her hair pulled back in a loose ponytail, she looked less honky-tonk angel and more rural housewife.

I had played for tips earlier that evening, so I held my guitar in one hand as I pulled Jolene to me with my free arm. I kissed her, but she pushed me away and said, "Wash off that stink before you go doing that again."

I stripped off my western-style jacket and the rest of my clothes before showering, and I exited the bathroom a while later wearing only a white towel wrapped around my waist. She had scrambled eggs, toast, and whiskey-laced coffee waiting, and I dug into it. Between bites I told her about my encounter with Grover Dahl.

"He ain't been the same since he came home," she said. "Hell, nobody who came back from Korea's the same, but most of them still have all their parts."

"What's he mean about the money?"

"Redemption?" she asked. "He don't talk about it, but Grover was one of the first casualties during the invasion. He never even fired his weapon."

"So how do you know?"

"Crystal told me all about it. We've been friends since grade school and never kept secrets from one another, or so I thought. She made me swear not to tell anyone."

"So why tell me?"

"She's gone," Jolene said. "She's never coming back."

"I still don't—"

"Everybody was feeling sorry for Grover," Jolene said, "so he had to prove he wasn't less of a man because he lost his legs.

With a couple of his high-school buddies as his muscle, Grover took control of all the gambling operations around these parts. He uses Elroy's place to turn the money legit, and—"

"—and Crystal knew all that?"

"Oh, the money made her happy," Jolene said, "but all the money couldn't make him whole. She wanted something Grover couldn't give her, and she found it almost every Saturday night."

"She used me—and you helped her."

"I never once heard you complain."

I pushed the last of my eggs onto the last of my toast and stuffed everything into my mouth. "So why did she leave when she did?"

"The timing was right," Jolene said. "Grover and his boys were over in Mertz, Elroy cut out early 'cause he was getting some, and Crystal knew the safe was full. It wasn't a coincidence she left when she did. She'd spent months planning for it."

"Where was she going?"

"The big city. Any big city. With her looks and Grover's money, she figured she'd be set."

I figured she was right, but I didn't say so.

"She left something behind," Jolene continued. "When I realized you weren't leaving, I held onto it. You've been good to me, these last couple of months, so—"

Jolene disappeared into her bedroom and returned with my guitar case, no worse for having been stolen. After fitting my Martin D-28 inside the case, I closed the lid, snapped the latches, and patted the case as if it were my baby.

"You weren't important to Crystal, she just used you for that," Jolene explained as she pointed at the guitar case. "You weren't the first guitar player she screwed, so no one would think you were any different than the other one-night stands she's had since Grover came home. And she always carried the guitar case when they walked over to the Dixie, so people 'round here got used to seeing her carrying one."

I put the pieces together. "She used it to carry the money she took from the safe, but something must have gone wrong," I said. "My guitar case is still here. So, where's Crystal Dahl?"

"It don't matter where she is, Ernie," Jolene said as she loosened my towel and let it drop to the floor. "What matters is what you do next."

The Dew Drop Inn was open every night, most weeknights serving drinkers with no place better to be. The weekends were the busiest, when live bands brought in hard-drinking two-steppers seeking temporary companionship more than dance partners, and Elroy served burgers, fries, and onion rings in addition to bottled beer and hard liquor straight-up. By last call, the floors were littered with cigarette butts and sticky with spilled drinks, and the restrooms were testaments to the incredibly poor aim of urinating drunks. Sometimes bourbon and burgers didn't mix, and the smell of expelled meals only added to the funk of the place. In the wee hours of the morning, after Elroy, Jolene, and the part-time cook cleaned up the dishes and stray bottles, I hosed down the concrete dance floor, scrubbed the toilets, and emptied all the trash receptacles. I had not worked so hard since leaving my parents' hardscrabble farm when I was sixteen, and by the time the sun rose on Sunday morning I regretted every bad decision I had ever made.

And I had made plenty. They usually involved whiskey and women because I'd never been able to turn down a bottle or a blonde, and they both lied to me. Whiskey made every woman a beauty queen, and every woman promised to love me—at least until daylight. Jolene was different, or so I thought. She hadn't promised me anything but hot meals, warm embraces, and an audience for stories about my previous life in Nashville. She even insisted that she would get us out of Chicken Junction if I would stick with her long enough.

* * *

I wore my western-style jacket—black with red roses embroidered near the shoulders—over a white shirt and black string
tie, black slacks, and black cowboy boots when I returned to the
stage at the Dew Drop Inn the following Tuesday night. Jolene
didn't work Tuesdays because there were barely enough drinkers
to keep Elroy busy behind the stick. I left my guitar case open on
the edge of the stage to collect tips, and I launched into a Hank
Williams tune the half-dozen patrons would recognize. I followed
that with songs by Ernest Tubb, Lefty Frizzell, and Buster Brown.
Throughout the first set, I played a mix of recent hits, old favorites, and hillbilly tunes I'd learned at my grandfather's knee, and
I started the next set the same way.

Grover Dahl wheeled into the honky-tonk halfway through
my second set, his Brahman-bull-sized cowboys at his side. They
watched me perform "If You've Got the Money, I've Got the
Time," and then disappeared into the back. At the end of the
set, Lucky caught my attention, escorted me to the office, and
made me sit in a hard wooden chair on the visitor side of the
desk so that I was eye-level with Grover.

"Where'd you get the guitar case?"

I realized my mistake. I shouldn't have taken the case to the
tonk. I said, "Jolene had it."

The ugly cowboy left the office.

"How'd she get it?"

"She didn't say, and I didn't ask."

"You think Jolene had your case all these months and didn't
tell you?"

"Well, I don't think your wife came back just to return it."

"You have a smart mouth, Ernie, but life's easy for you. You
haven't lost what I've lost."

I didn't know if he meant his legs or his wife or both, so I
said nothing, and we stared at each other for a moment before
he let me return to the stage in time for my third set.

I wasn't surprised when, halfway through it, Lucky returned
with Jolene and dragged her through the Dew Drop. I was sur-

prised several minutes later when both cowboys came barreling out of the back and disappeared through the front door.

At the end of my last set, I scooped six dollars and twelve cents—most of it coins—out of my case and shoved it into my pocket. Then I nestled my D-28 into place, closed the lid, and snapped the latches into place. I had just hefted it off the stage when Jolene stomped across the dance floor, pressed her breasts against my chest, and forced me backward.

She glared up into my eyes. "I shouldn't'a give you the case," she said through gritted teeth. "I didn't think you'd be stupid enough to bring it here where Grover could see you got it back."

I grabbed Jolene's arm and walked her outside. We were standing next to Crystal Dahl's Thunderbird, still parked in the lot long after her disappearance. "So, what'd you tell Grover?"

"I told him what I'm telling you," she said. "Crystal called me that morning to pick her up, said her car wouldn't start. Once I got here, she put that guitar case in the back seat of my car—that and a travel bag—climbed in with it and told me to take her over to Quarryville where she could catch the bus to Dallas. Well, I watched her in the rearview as she took cash money out of your guitar case and stuffed it in her travel bag. When we got to Quarryville she gave me a twenty for my gas and the last I saw her she was getting on a bus." She held up her hand, palm toward me. "That's the God's honest truth."

Every relationship I'd ever had was based on a lie, so I knew a lie when I heard one. I lowered my voice. "I don't think it is," I said. "I don't think Crystal ever got on a bus, no matter what you had Grover and his boys believing, and when his boys come back, he's going to know you lied to him."

"I'll be gone by then," she said.

"And just where are you planning to go?"

"As far from this Godforsaken town as fifteen grand will take me."

Grover quietly rolled out of the Dew Drop, and he sat in his wheelchair behind Jolene. He had the snub-nosed .38 in his hand but it wasn't quite pointing at either of us. "If you've got the money, honey—"

When he spoke, Jolene spun around to face him. "That bitch was planning to keep it all," Jolene said. "After all I'd done for her, after all—"

"You killed my wife for the money?"

"She promised that we'd leave together, that'd she'd take care of me, but—"

Grover swung the .38 a few inches to the left. "So, where's the money?"

"My trailer."

"And my wife? Where is she?"

"I dumped her body down Johnson's well," Jolene said.

Grover squeezed the trigger. Jolene's eyes widened with surprise and then dulled with pain as she collapsed against me. "We never had a chance," she told me. "This town, this town, this—"

I lowered her to the ground.

"Was she good?" Grover asked. He motioned with the barrel of the snub-nosed revolver. "Was she good in bed?"

Uncertain what he wanted to hear, I said, "Not as good as your wife. No woman could be."

I thought Grover was going to shoot me, too, but he dug in his pocket, tossed me the keys to Crystal's Thunderbird, and said, "Get out of here."

After putting my guitar case in the passenger seat, I climbed behind the wheel. When I keyed the ignition, nothing happened. I popped the hood, discovered that someone had disconnected the positive battery cable, and I reattached it. Then I drove away without looking back. I had a lot of time to think as I drove, and I should have used it, but thinking had never been my strong suit.

I had just wheeled into Texarkana, headed for the Arkansas border on my way back to Nashville, when a Texas Highway Patrol officer pulled me over. I was driving a stolen car, covered in Jolene's blood, with evidence in the trunk that the Thunderbird had been used to transport a dead body. No matter how many times I told my story, the words of a blackout drunk didn't carry the same weight as those of a legless Korean War veteran.

When Buster Brown and His Big Hat Band performed for the prisoners at the Texas State Penitentiary at Huntsville a few years later, I was in the audience. I thought about my one night with Crystal, but mostly I thought about Jolene. She had the money, honey, but I'm doing the time.

PLEASURE GONE BAD

Jonathan Brown

11:30 p.m.

"Welcome to the *Country Cast*, the west coast's hottest country music podcast. I'm your host Sherry Keefer and I'm backstage at the Star Corral Honky-Tonk Bar in El Segundo, California. I have the pleasure of sitting down with lead singer and amazing harp player Duke Suggs of Busted Saddle, who pretty much have a residency here. Duke, so glad you could join us."

"The pleasure's mine Sherry," Duke said.

"We only have a few minutes, people, because Duke is actually on a break between sets, so we're super honored to have him."

"Pleasure's still mine Sherry and, might I add, you're much prettier in person than on social media."

"Oh, you silver-tongued devil, you," Sherry smiled. "They warned me about you."

"Well, how dare they," Duke said. "I just call 'em as I see 'em."

"For those of you in podcast land, it's not just his Southern drawl, but his eyes are dreamy, too. But on to you: congratulations to you and Busted Saddle. You guys are killing it. You've been added to the Stagecoach Festival and, rumor has it, a tour with Carrie Underwood is in play?"

"Yes, well, we're truly blessed."

"I'm sure the good peeps here at the Star Corral are gonna miss you."

"Aw, I miss them already. But, I tell you what, we'll be back. 'Cause L.A. is home."

"Okay, I'm jumping right in, like I do."

"Let's do it," Duke smiled.

"I've interviewed Darius Rucker a few times now and he's not shy in mentioning his early struggles being a black musician in the country music world. How's it been for the soon-to-be famous Duke Suggs?"

"Well, I must say, Miss Keefer, country and western fans are the greatest fans on earth," Duke ended the sentence with a wink.

"What a diplomat. But seriously no problems?"

"Oh, sure, in some of the clubs in the early days but once them folks heard my velvet tone we seemed to bond over the music. And for every bad person or racist there were ten kind, warm-hearted folks," he paused. "Of all colors. Love beats hate every time, Sherry."

Duke was an expert at reading people, always had been. He could tell Sherry found him cocky, maybe even arrogant, but still, she was attracted to him. And that's what mattered. He wondered if he could land her after the show. A few more minutes with her and he'd know if the door would be open or not. He hoped so—Sherry Keefer was fine as all-git-out!

Just then the brim of Steady Pete the keyboard player's leather Bullhide hat poked into the green room.

"Sorry boss, but we're on in five," he said to Duke before feeding Sherry a big smile. "Big fan of the podcast by the way."

"Why, thank you. Ladies and gentlemen, Steady Pete," Sherry said. "Well, I guess that's it for now. Duke Suggs, thank you so much for the window. Maybe we could continue after the show—the interview I mean," she added blushing at seeing the way Duke looked at her. She turned off the hand-held recorder.

"You are a troublemaker, Mister Suggs," she said, wrapping up her portable gear.

"Do you like trouble, Miss Keefer? Because if you do, we could—"

Davey Boy, the drummer, hurried into the room and practically fell over. A drumstick dropped from his hand, bounced off his cowboy boot and rolled toward Sherry. "Sorry guys. Hey, Duke, we're on in two and I can't find Little Steve," he said, breathless.

"That's not like Mr. Punctual. Little Steve's our bass player," Duke said by way of explanation to Sherry. Rising from his seat, Duke said, "Will you excuse me?"

"Of course," Sherry said, extending a hand. Duke gently took the hand and pulled her into a hug. He was not surprised he liked the way she felt.

"We're big huggers in this band, Sherry. Thanks for the interview. Get yourself a couple drinks at the bar, my tab. I hope you stick around—sincerely," he said, tossing the patented wink her way.

"Um, yeah, sure. Maybe. Thank you."

Flustered. Got 'er!

He turned to his drummer. "Davey Boy, let's go huntin'." Before leaving the room, Duke pinched the brim of his black-felt Stetson and gave Sherry a quick nod. She forced herself not to smile too hard. Duke had seen it a thousand times before.

11:43 p.m.

Duke and Davey Boy walked into the club and approached the stage where Jen, the sound person, was swapping out some microphone cables.

"Hey Jen, ya seen Little Steve?"

"Mr. Punctual? Nope. It ain't like him neither. Try the can. I saw him scarfing down some of our chili and I wouldn't feed that shit to my ex-husband, if you catch my drift."

"Don't lie to me girl, you'd feed him two servings with a

smile while you sipped tequila," Duke said.

Jen put a finger to her lips, "Shh, true, just don't tell anyone."

"Promise. Davey Boy, hit the can will ya? I'll check the back bar."

Davey Boy nodded and did his best to weave through the throng. Duke made a hard left from the stage and moved along it toward the smaller of the two giant bars. The smaller bar was where band members hung out if they didn't want the big bar's traffic.

"Duke, sounding good tonight," said a pockmarked kid in his twenties wearing an oversized Stetson.

"Thanks, man."

"You got any Zac Brown Band coming up?"

"We got 'Chicken Fried' on the way, sit tight now, ya hear."

"Awesome!"

Duke cleared the dance floor section and strode to the back bar and was greeted by Drunk Tina on her usual perch.

"Duke, you sexy mutha—fu-fucker," she hiccupped. "Buy me a shot?"

"Someday I'm sure. Ya seen Little Steve?"

Drunk Tina knitted up her brow.

"My bass player," Duke said, wondering why he'd bothered.

She blinked twice and raised her eyebrows and hiccupped, "Yesh, outside, the back, he went, went outside."

Duke headed in the direction of the rear exit because as drunk as Drunk Tina got, she was surprisingly reliable. He bumped into Davey Boy on the way.

"He wasn't in the can, Duke," he said, worried.

"I gathered from the fact it's just you and not the both o' y'all. Check the big bar and ask Casey or Chuck if they saw him. I'll check his ride. Text me if you get 'im."

Duke popped his head out the back door and found Casey, the bar-back having a smoke.

"Duke, how they hangin' bra?"

"'Bout where they should be. Ya seen Little Steve?"

"'Bout ten minutes ago yeah. Hey ain't you guys supposed to be on now?"

Duke gave him a look.

"Right, that's why you're looking for him, duh. Sorry."

"Was he with anyone?"

"Huh? Ah, no."

The hesitation of a liar: you say 'huh' even though you heard me...

"He was doin' blow wasn't he?" Duke said.

Duke could see Casey didn't want to get dragged into anything and Duke didn't blame the kid.

"It's okay, buddy. Look, if he comes back out here tell him to get his ass to the stage."

"Sure, will do, Duke."

11:58 p.m.

A quick check of Little Steve's Dodge Durango turned up empty. Duke checked his phone—no text from his drummer.

Fuck.

Duke asked the bouncers at the front door and they were no help either. Then Duke had an idea.

I fucking hope not.

In the basement of the Star Corral were an old furnace, some leaky pipes, and a tiny twelve-by-fourteen-foot room that once served as the original green room for the bands. It was pretty much storage and rat shit nowadays. Sometimes players from various bands, and staff members for that matter, used the room to get off a quick romp or do drugs harder than weed. Duke feared that his bass player might be engaged in a secret rendezvous with Chuck the bartender. It's not that the dingy green room would be their room of choice, but Little Steve had a boyfriend who happened to be in the club that night. And Duke knew Little Steve and Chuck had a thing on the side.

Duke wished his bass player had never told him about the relationship. Oh, well, he thought, as he was about to enter the dank room. If Little Steve was inside getting his rocks off, Duke was going to kill him for holding up the show.

He pounded three times hard on the door. "Yo, Little Steve, you in there? You better get your ass upstairs if you are. And I'm docking you twenty-five bucks if—"

The door inched open.

Like a bad horror movie...

"Little Steve?"

The room was empty. "Fuck."

Duke turned to go when he noticed one of the four old-school locker doors was ajar. It shouldn't have bumped him, but it did. He strode without hesitation and hauled it open.

"Fuck me!"

Duke was looking at his bass player. He was dead and gone with his pants around his ankles and shirtless. A cowboy bolo tie was attached to a bass guitar string and cinched tight around his neck. The bolo was tied in a noose around the neck while the bass string—E string to be exact—was attached to the bolo by way of a Stevedore box braid knot. Duke's father's only passion outside of being a cop was fishing. And by age ten Duke knew more fishing knots than he cared to. He cringed at the memories of numerous surprise quizzes his old man had given him. Duke ignored the Stetson as it tumbled out of the locker at his boots. Little Steve's neck was red, his skin pale and his eyes wide. Duke slowly put a finger to his neck but he knew the pulse had quit at least thirty minutes earlier.

"Fuck a Sunday duck, little buddy. Did you really need to get off that bad?"

Duke was no expert, but he'd seen documentaries and heard plenty of folklore: Little Steve had been engaged in autoerotic asphyxiation and accidentally killed himself.

Poor fucker.

Duke was about to close the locker door and call the cops

when something bumped him just like the locker door's being open had. He stared at his dead friend. Something wasn't right but he couldn't nail it down...until...

"Son of a bitch." He stared a moment longer then closed the door. With the cuff of his crisp dress shirt, he wiped down the locker door handle as well as the entry door's stained copper knob and climbed back up the stairs. Duke was pissed. Someone had killed his friend and Duke was going to find out who did it before the law came crawling all over it.

12:08 a.m.

When he got upstairs, he walked past the dart game area and mechanical bull corral and beelined for the big bar in search of Todd the bar manager.

"Hey, Todd, I gotta slight problem."

"What's up? Did the podcast run long? You guys are supposed to be up now aren't ya?"

"Pod—oh, yeah, no." He'd forgotten all about the interview. A quick flash of Sherry's supple lips, cleavage and tiny waist jumped into his vision. He forced it aside. "Listen, I'm gonna do a short acoustic set with my guitar player, just like four or five tunes. Then we'll get back at it after a short break."

"Whatever works for you guys," Todd smiled. "We're just happy you're here."

Good old Todd, God love him. "Thanks, man."

"Just don't forget us little people when you're famous," Todd said.

"Not a chance," Duke said, breaking away. Scanning the room, he found Cutt, the guitar player, Davey Boy, and Steady Pete huddled around Davey Boy's drum set. A dozen two-steppers danced around the floor in front of the stage to the canned music. Duke moved in their direction but was blocked by a tall thin man in his mid-sixties. He had an easy manner about him.

"Duke Suggs, I presume," he said in a bass-baritone voice. He wore Wrangler jeans, black Justin boots, a crisp, light blue cowboy shirt, and a black Stetson that'd seen plenty of dusty acreage.

"Yes, sir," Duke said politely, hoping to get done with the gentleman quickly.

"Allow me to buy you a shot," he said, handing Duke a shot glass and clinking it off his own.

"I suppose it'd be rude not to accept," Duke said. "What are we drinking to?"

"Your band's tempos. My wife and I scuff up some serious hardwood out here and the tempos are everything."

"Ah, yes, I seem to remember a sweet two-step, a silky-smooth cha-cha and a lean-and-mean boot scoot. Y'all are a pleasure to watch from up there."

"Wow, you see all that when you're singing, huh? Crazy."

Duke thanked him for the shot and gathered the troops.

"Fellas, Little Steve's indisposed at the moment so Cutt, you and I are gonna hit 'bout five numbers until we sort this out. The rest o' y'all take a short break but don't be gettin' too loaded now, ya hear?"

The band members, with the exception of Davey Boy, seemed satisfied, but Davey Boy was the worrier in the band and was rarely satisfied. Duke needed the short set to run the mystery down in his head and to also satisfy his contract with the club—give the people what they want. Little Steve's death was definitely a murder. As far as Duke knew, only staff and band members knew of the old green room. That ruled out hundreds of patrons in the club as suspects. His father would say everyone was a suspect, but Duke wasn't his father, nor did he have time to canvas the club. Once the cops were in the fold that'd be it for Duke. Hell, he'd probably be a suspect for a time. The killer could have left the bar, but Duke didn't think so, although he wasn't sure why.

Back to work.

"How do y'all feel about this bar, do you love it 'er what?"
"Yes," the crowd cheered.
"I said do y'all love it?" louder this time.
"Yes!"
"Well, all right then. Here's a little Toby Keith number for ya."
Duke barely needed to sing as "I Love This Bar" is a big audience participation song. Duke spotted Nigel, Little Steve's boyfriend, sitting on a barstool at the small bar. With two drinks in front of him, his head swiveled in all directions and he constantly checked his phone. Poor feller, Duke thought. His boyfriend ain't coming for that drink.

Duke joined the crowd for the final chorus. He and Cutt ran through two fast numbers and then brought it back around to "Letter To My Daughters," a ballad in three-four-time, by Uncle Kracker. A quick applause went up as the dancers eased into the waltz. Duke had sung the song so many times he put his mind on autopilot to think about solving his friend's murder, only his mind went to his father.

Larry Suggs was Texas P.D. for twenty years before being killed in the line of duty. He and his partner thought they'd gotten everybody out of the meth house but there was one straggler behind a .357 Magnum Desert Eagle. Five of the nine rounds went into his father's body. Larry had hung on forty-six minutes, the tough old bird.

Duke was on track to follow in his dad's footsteps but getting caught sleeping with the firearms instructor's wife while in the academy queered the deal for Duke. He didn't really care. He'd always known that it was music that got him out of bed in the morning. On the other hand, his dear old dad had practically run his son out of Texas. Duke hooked up with a band headed west. They posted up in Los Angeles. For six months it was gravy until Duke did what Duke does, and that little backup singer who always wore Daisy Dukes and bustiers was too much for him to handle. So, when she started flirting with Duke, he flirted right back. The singer's husband—who happened to be the drummer—

caught the vibe and fired Duke. When the hot little singer stopped by Duke's dumpy apartment to apologize, one thing led to another and the singer's apology lasted three full days before they came up for air.

"This was a big mistake," she said when it was over.

"Day one, two or three, sweetheart?"

"You're an asshole," she said, slamming his door. A minute and a half later she stormed back in for one last, fast, and hard round, then slapped him across his face and left for good this time.

Duke was pleasantly surprised by the vast size of L.A.'s country music scene. He took a couple of hired gigs until eventually forming Busted Saddle. That was eighteen months ago and he hadn't looked back since...until...now that his bass player had been murdered.

He shook the history loose and finished out the song, holding a long, high note that the crowd ate up like barbecued brisket.

"Much obliged beautiful people. We gon' take a short one and be right back. Don't go nowhere now, ya hear?"

12:29 p.m.

Duke pulled up to the bar to rap with Chuck, the bartender, and former side action of his bass player.

"When did you last see Little Steve?"

"Fuck me, keep your voice down. His boyfriend Nigel is here, dude. I wish you'd never found out."

"That makes two of us. It don't answer my question though."

Chuck leaned his chunky forearms on the bar and loud-whispered. "Listen, it's over. I'm done with the kinky fucker; I'm through being someone's secret, okay?"

"Are you telling or convincing?" Duke asked.

Chuck pulled his arms off the bar and folded them across his chest.

"I saw him like forty-five or an hour ago. He tried his shit with me, totally not respecting boundaries—look, ninety minutes ago. There's your answer." He turned on his boot heel and moved down the bar.

Duke stopped by Nigel next and ran the same question by him. He was agitated—hadn't seen Little Steve in at least an hour.

"I think he's cheating on me," he said, fighting back tears. "Is he? You'd tell me if he was, right? I know you're friends, but you want his relationship to be healthy, don't you?"

"Come on Nigel. I don't get into other people's relationships."

"I bet a hundred wives tell a different story."

"That's fair," Duke said, recalling a million snippets of flashbacks all at once. "But I just need to know when you last saw him and who he was with?"

"He was talking with Drunk Tina for a minute, although I don't know why she's such a—"

"That was an hour ago or so?"

Nigel nodded, then took a gentle sip from what Duke figured was an Appletini.

"Good lookin' out, buddy," Duke said, turning to leave, but Nigel clutched his wrist.

"Seriously, is he cheating? Just tell me." The tears weren't staying in his eyes anymore.

"No, he's not."

Because he's downstairs jammed in a closet like a pretzel...

Duke pried loose and strode to the small bar and ordered two shots of Jack Daniel's. He slammed the first one and was about to down the second.

"You look like you needed that," the woman beside him said.

Duke turned to the voice. "Sherry, hey."

"Are you all right?"

Damn she's fine...that mouth.

"Come with me," he said. "I'll get you a fresh one when we get back," he said, nodding toward her drink.

"Normally you buy the girl the drink first," Sherry said,

stepping off the barstool. As he grabbed her arm, she resisted, but only slightly. He tugged a little harder.

"It'll be fine, trust me. I need to show you something."

He led her through the crowd, ignoring fans that wanted his attention. She allowed him to interlace his fingers with hers. After squeezing past the mechanical bull area and past two couples playing darts, they were at the old back staircase.

"Watch your step," Duke said as he led her down the narrow stairs.

"Oh, hell no," Sherry said when she entered the dank basement room. "I heard you like to play but this girl's got class, buddy. I'm outta here."

Duke watched her ass as it moved toward the door. He almost looked too long because she was nearly out of the room.

"Wait, please."

She stopped. Pissed…but looked amazing when angry. Duke walked to the locker.

"There's been an accident. Please don't scream. Oh, and brace yourself," he said and slowly opened the door. The podcaster's eyes grew wide. She pitched forward and put a hand to her mouth.

"What in the fuck, Duke? Why would you show—"

"Because I trust you," he said. "And I need your help."

Duke slowly closed the door and fastened the latch, then repeated wiping off the prints.

"Listen. I know this looks like a masturbation accident but it's not. He was murdered. And," he paused. "He was my friend."

"Okay, you know what, I need to get outta here, I'm gonna be—"

Duke escorted her out the door. She bent over but held it together. Duke sat her on the steps and ran his plan down for her. It took three minutes to get her on board.

"Thanks, sweetheart. I know it seems fucked but we're doing the right thing."

Back in the club they stood by the small bar.

"Folks call her Drunk Tina. I need you to keep an eye on her."

"What am I looking for exactly?" Sherry asked, straightening her spine.

"Anytime something bugs me or sets off my radar, I call it a bump. Just watch and if something bumps you, make a note of it, cool?"

"Yes, and—"

Duke slipped a hand to the small of her back, pulled her in and kissed her hard on the lips.

"Sorry, sweetheart, that just wasn't containable no more," Duke said. "You were about to say?"

"Hmm, I sure don't remember now," she smiled. "Now go away, I've got work to do," she said, heading to a barstool three down from Drunk Tina.

Duke was forced to shake two people's hands, do a shot of Jack, take a group photo and accept two different numbers from two different groupies.

Country music chicks—yes, please!

Todd, the bar manager, hovered near the coffee machine.

"Hey, good buddy, when did you last see my bass player?" Duke asked.

"Hour or so. Heading out back with Chuck," he said, lowering his voice.

"Really?"

"One went one way around the dance floor and the other went the long way, then they skipped out the door separately. You know about them, right?"

"Not by choice," Duke said. "So they tried the discreet approach, that what you sayin'?"

Todd nodded. That meant Chuck had lied about seeing Little Steve. Why? Duke went in search of Casey at the bar back and found him in the kitchen, emptying out his tray.

"Yo, Casey."

Casey's shoulders dropped when he saw Duke.

"Don't worry, I'm not putting you in the soup, just one last question. I know Little Steve went outside to do lines but when I asked you if he was alone, you lied. Was he with Chuck? Head nod yes—shake for no and I'm out."

Casey nodded slowly. Duke got up to leave.

"They did a line off the back of each other's hands and then went at each other."

"That it?"

"By that time, I fucked off down the alley. I didn't need to see—"

"Got it. And thanks. But, Casey."

"Yeah?"

"You were just supposed to nod or shake your head. What's with the full-length movie, bud?"

The kid looked worried. Duke pulled ten dollars out of his wallet and handed it to the bar back.

"Relax. Buy yourself a shot, kid."

12:42 a.m.

"Whatta we got?" Duke asked Sherry.

"Precious little. But she sure can put 'em away. Occasionally she tries to get a conversation going, other times she rambles to herself."

"Any bumps?"

"Maybe."

"Gimme."

"At one point she started texting. I slid in behind her but I couldn't get too close, didn't want to blow my cover," she smiled weakly.

"You see who she texted?"

"No, sorry. But," she paused. "She never fumbled or dropped her phone. She texts at a million miles an hour with a steady hand and I couldn't do that liquored up. It's like she wasn't drunk at all."

"Darlin', that's a bump." Duke smiled.

Sherry smiled back, "Are you a singer or a P.I.?"

"Daddy was a cop."

"Ah," she said.

"Do me a favor. Google Tina Simms, Nigel Jefferson, and Chuck the bartender. His real name is Charlie Whitney."

Duke told her who Nigel was. Sherry put the names into her phone notes as Duke went through the list.

"Look for bumps, connections, anything you think is useful."

She looked up when she was done. "I feel bad I'm having fun doing this. Your poor friend," she said, creasing up her eyebrows.

"Plenty o' time for tears later."

Sherry got up on her toes and kissed Duke softly.

"I got the jump on you this time," she smiled as she pulled away.

"That you did," Duke said.

12:52 a.m.

Duke gathered Busted Saddle together in the main floor modern-day green room. The band members were clearly concerned about Little Steve.

"Where the fuck's Little Steve, Duke? You been running all over this fucking bar like—"

"We got one more set to do and Little Steve ain't doin' it with us. Steady Pete, you're gonna cover bass with your left hand. I'll explain everything later. For now, the show must go on. We get paid, go home and start rehearsing for the tour."

Duke was like a police chief that wouldn't take any further questions from the press. The band grumbled but fell in line.

"Bullet the Dwight Yoakam tune and we'll end with 'Chicken Fried,' 'cause I promised a guy."

The set was seamless. Steady Pete covered the bass parts like a champ. Holding the grief down deep in his gut, Duke entertained as if his friend were beside him on stage.

After the set, Duke instructed the band to meet him in the old green room. When they bellyached, he put fire into his light brown eyes. The Saddle complied. He stopped by Sherry and took all she'd gotten from her search, then sent her downstairs to join the band. Duke went behind the small bar and grabbed a bottle of Jameson and swung it back and forth in front of Drunk Tina.

"Buy you that drink now, sweetheart?"

Eyes wide, she slid off her stool with ease.

1:29 a.m.

"Thank you all for coming down to this shithole. I'm sorry to do it this way but Little Steve is dead."

Duke gave the group a moment to fall apart.

"Here's the breakdown. Little Steve, while in a relationship with Nigel, was seeing Chuck on the side. Chuck ended the relationship tonight but not before a goodbye romp and cocaine in the alley."

"And you know this how?" Davey Boy asked.

Duke kept going. "This is all confirmed by Casey and Chuck, sort of. At some point after our second set, when I was doing the podcast, Little Steve came down here and was killed."

Duke shushed the group.

"Question is who would want sweet Little Steve dead? After I discovered the body I asked for Sherry's help."

"Sherry? Before us?" Steady Pete said. "That's fucked up."

"I had to clear you guys first. Anyway, Sherry searched the internet for me and made a discovery about Drunk Tina."

All eyes went to Drunk Tina, who in that moment, seemed oblivious as she took a large pull on the Jameson bottle.

"This ain't gon' be pretty, Saddle-ites."

Duke's voice cracked, and he could feel tears forming in the back part of his eyes as he opened the locker. Duke gave the group a solid five minutes to go through all of the necessary emotions.

"At this point I'd like all of you to head back upstairs and call the cops. Send 'em down here."

The group moved as a herd, squeezing from an open range into a tiny corral gate.

"Tina, Sherry, hang back, please. Thanks."

2:03 a.m.

"Tina, the three of us know cops are coming for you, so spill it. Why'd you kill my friend?"

Drunk Tina held Duke's gaze with a smirk that Duke knew was more sober than it appeared. Her body began to shake with a low guttural laugh. Duke wanted to kill her in that moment but knew a jail cell would be punishment enough.

"Sherry dug up some old photos on social of you and Little Steve. I knew my boy was into the kink, but I didn't take him for bisexual."

"He used to be straight," she said, "and loved me the way I loved him."

Her look drifted back to the pages of history. "We were amazing together, always laughing. We had the most amazing sex one night. I mean he got me to do things—anyway, in the morning—'I'm gay' he says—'I realize now that I'm done with women.' Can you believe that? I came three fucking times and then—" She didn't finish. Duke brought her back to the present.

"Tell me about tonight, Tina."

With a heavy sigh and light tears in her eyes she opened up.

"I catch all your shows and tonight I see him fucking around with Chuck, breaking Nigel's heart like he did mine," she said. "He's a fucking forest fire scorching the earth, one person at a time. He's why I started boozing so hard in the first place." She pulled a pack of smokes from her purse. Duke lit one for her. She took a deep drag and followed it with a heavy pull on the Jameson.

"So, tonight I tell him who I am. My hair was totally different back then. I'd had a sort of pixie, dyed pink with shitty bangs. Plus, I wear color contacts and didn't dress cowgirl back then. Anyway," she said, blowing a smoke ring, "he seemed happy to see me. Charming fucker totally disarmed me."

"How'd you get him down here?"

She went back to her purse and pulled out a bag of coke. "Tony Montana's Yayo. He's like a dog to peanut butter with this shit."

"So what went wrong?" Duke asked, managing his temper.

"He grabs his bass case. 'I gotta change a string,' he says. We come down here, do a line and shoot the shit. He starts changing out the string. Problem is, he goes on about how happy he is being gay, how he loves the community, and—" She paused, closed her eyes, and put a palm to her forehead. Butting the cig under her heel, she hoisted the Jameson and downed four fingers' worth.

She burped and said, "It's like he was grinding his happiness in my face with the heel of his fucking Cody James, ya know? And seeing him run around upstairs with Chuck, while poor Nigel—"

"I know, Nigel was beside himself, waiting for Little Stevie like a Labrador waits for his daddy to come home after his workday," Duke said. "I considered him for the murder, but his agitation was genuine."

"Then he asks me to toss out the spent bass string and I was about to," she paused. Once again, her look floated away.

"But then I got behind the cheating, happy fucker and—"

She let it hang. Duke looked to Sherry and noticed tears in her eyes. He felt bad conscripting her into the alliance.

"So you strangled him, then shoved him into the locker and made it look like pleasure gone bad."

Drunk Tina nodded.

"Darlin' you ain't but a hundred and twenty pounds in a rainstorm? How the hell d'ya overpower him and get 'im in there?"

With eyes downcast, she unbuttoned her checkered blouse and pulled the sleeves off her shoulders to the elbows.

"Son of a bitch," Duke said seeing her muscular shoulders and traps. Even her forearms were ripped and corded.

"Cross-Fit, six days a week for the last six years. I booze and I train. That's it. I could lift you over my head without blinking an eye, Duke."

"I reckon so."

2:22 a.m.

The three of them could hear footsteps descending the stairs. The cops.

"I could kill you for killing my friend, but jail will have to do."

Drunk Tina nodded, then killed the last of the Jameson.

"I got one for you, Duke. How'd you know it wasn't an accident?"

"Well, I ain't into the kink like Little Steve was, but there ain't a man I know pulls his pants down to the boots when he wants ta', you know. That and the knot is a version of the Stevedore—the box braid knot.

"Sherry," Duke said. "What does that knot make you think of?"

Sherry squinted a moment before answering. "It looks like a French hair braid."

"Exactly, and few men know anything about the braid. Women on the other hand..."

"Why didn't you run?" Sherry asked.

"I'm sloshed," she said with a shrug of her shoulders.

The door swung open and two officers walked in.

"Besides," she said. "Duke solved this fucker in under three hours and he ain't even a cop. How far you think I'd get?"

"What have we got?" asked the officer in charge.

"Murder victim in that locker. Murderer in that chair," Duke said as he pointed to Drunk Tina. "And the confession recorded on Miss Keefer's cell phone."

Sherry held up her phone as proof. The younger cop used a pen, lifted the locker latch and opened the door. The older cop approached Drunk Tina, who held out her hands in surrender. Duke removed his Stetson, eyed his dead friend, and let the tears flow.

"Buddy, we played together, sang together and got drunk together. And y'all can bet we'll do it again on down the road. Until then," he said, clearing his throat, "rest in peace, buddy. Rest in peace."

THE ROSE

Stacy Woodson

Red wasn't sure who pulled the gun first—the clown or the bartender.

Frankly, he didn't care.

He was pissed.

Not about the guns. They didn't bother him so much. Hell, he carried one himself. It was Texas after all, and part of the culture, a way of life. No, he was pissed that during the ruckus the bartender had knocked over a perfectly good bottle of whiskey.

He watched the brown liquid pool on the bar while he debated whether or not to get involved. Breaking up fights wasn't why he'd been hired to be here.

"Where the hell is Jimmy?" the clown demanded.

Red considered the Colt Python strapped to his hip and sized up the clown.

Man had come straight from the circuit, Red figured, judging by the dusty jeans and barely washed-off rodeo paint. He'd be fatigued. And then there was the way he was holding the Berretta—gangster style, safety still on.

Man didn't have a lick of sense about him. Hell, anyone who taunted a bull for a living didn't.

Red didn't need the Python.

Two strides were all it would take.

Maybe three.

Three would be enough to reach the clown and put him down. Red tested his hand, grimaced, the sprain still fresh from his last job.

The bartender and the clown continued to argue.

The band continued to play. Patrons continued to dance. A sea of cowboy hats, fringed shirts, and too-tight Wranglers glided over the sawdust-covered dance floor.

No one rushed outside, no one reached for their phone. Even the customers saddled up to the bar were still drinking like they'd seen this show before. No one seemed to take the clown seriously.

Maybe Red shouldn't either.

He ignored the wasted whiskey, went back to his beer—two pulls and it was empty. He wanted another. But the 12-gauge was still tucked against the bartender's shoulder.

The woman looked different in person, Red decided. Older than he'd expected—not physically. She was petite, slender. Her blond hair was cropped short, wavy. Styled in that youthful kind of way. No different from the picture Maddox had sent him.

The difference was in her eyes.

They looked weathered, hardened—a look that belonged to someone who'd seen things, done things.

Red considered intervening again. Not because the bartender couldn't handle her business. Do-si-do-ing with a drunk just took time, and he was ready for this dance to be over.

He was ready for another beer.

Hank Williams Jr. started to croon from the jukebox. Two seats down, an old-timer—a Marine veteran, Red guessed from the anchor and globe tattoo on his forearm—sipped his whiskey and sang along to "Family Tradition."

Red decided out of respect for the man's service, out of respect for Hank, he'd wait until the song was over before he intervened.

He pulled out a can of Copenhagen, flicked his wrist, packed the tobacco—the pop, pop, pop against the tin nearly as comforting as Hank. He placed a pinch under his lip and grabbed the empty beer bottle.

While he worked the tobacco, he rested his elbows on top of the bar. Under the yellowing urethane were pictures: weddings, dance contests, retirement gatherings, military welcome-home parties, and country singing legends before they'd hit their stride—all pictures taken here at The Rose. Most of them looked dated, old—at least fifty years—judging from the hairstyles, the clothing, and the younger versions of country artists that Red recognized.

He liked the history. There was a vibe about this place he liked, too.

Maybe it was the simplicity of it—the warehouse design, the weathered walls, the low ceilings. No carpets, no drapes, no prissy trappings. They served liquor and beer—not umbrella drinks or fruity cocktails or fern concoctions.

Maybe it was the smell of stale beer and sawdust, the dim lights, how the sound of the fiddles and steel guitars eased his jangled nerves.

Maybe it was the jar of pickled pigs feet behind the bar or the poster of Willie that did it for him. The place just felt genuine—like a worn pair of cowboy boots owned by real cowboys. The kind that worked on ranches. Not like the ones worn by city-slicker imports.

This was his kind of place.

These were his kind of people.

Fuck. He hated this job.

"Did ya hear me, Loretta?" The clown's voice was louder, boozy, pulling Red's focus back to the stupidity at the bar.

"It's like I told you before, Waylon," Loretta said, her tone measured, calm—like a schoolteacher dealing with an unruly kid. "My sorry excuse for a brother ain't here tonight." Her eyes darted past the clown toward the back of the honky-tonk where the bathrooms and an office were located.

The office door slivered open.

A taller, bulkier male version of Loretta peeked outside. She

193

locked eyes with her brother and shook her head, signaling him to stay there.

The inebriated clown didn't seem to notice, too busy trying to steady his feet. "I ain't no fool, Loretta. I done seen his truck in the parking lot."

"Of course, you saw Old Bluesides. I drove her today."

The shotgun remained against Loretta's shoulder.

The Berretta remained in Waylon's hand, still at that ridiculous cant.

Hank was winding down on the jukebox. Waylon wasn't.

"Oh, for Christ sakes," Red muttered. He pushed back from the bar and made his way toward the clown.

Two strides.

Red balled-up his hand.

Three.

He cocked back his arm.

But before Red could swing, Waylon's shoulders started to shake. The man began to cry—long, drawn-out sobs. He stumbled back, lost his footing.

Red reached out and caught the clown.

Tears mixed with paint ran down his cheeks. Red wasn't sure what bothered him more—how conflicted he felt or that now he cradled a goddamn clown.

He forced Waylon to his feet, catapulting him forward so hard that he nearly hit the bar. Then, Red took the Berretta, which the clown relinquished without a fight, either too devastated or too drunk to care.

"I'm sorry, Loretta," Waylon said between sobs, the reality of what he'd done seeming to suddenly hit him. "I ain't got no quarrel with you."

"I know, sugar." Loretta put the shotgun away.

While she rounded the bar, Red cleared the weapon. No bullets in the magazine, no round in the chamber. Clown was all hat, no cattle—which Loretta and the regulars must have known already. It would explain why they hadn't been alarmed by the ruckus.

Not sure what to do with the gun, Red considered handing it to Loretta, but she was still dealing with the clown.

"It's Evelyn, again," Waylon continued, voice still quavering.

"I suspected as much," Loretta said, standing in front of him now. She wrapped an arm around Waylon and walked him over to Red's empty barstool. He fell into the seat. "That girl doesn't bring out the best in you."

"Buckle bunnies ain't nothing but trouble, son," the old-timer chimed in.

Waylon sucked in a long snot-filled breath. The clown looked more like a kid now—still fighting through puberty—with his slight frame, his pimpled face, his wide-eyes.

"Clive is right," Loretta agreed. "Rodeo groupies and tender-hearted men ain't the best fit."

Waylon nodded. Or his head bobbed. Red wasn't sure. The kid was so drunk Red couldn't tell the difference.

Waylon laid his head on the bar and closed his eyes.

"Way that girl cats around." Clive shook his head. "Kid needs to grow a set and kick her to the curb."

"But I love her…" Waylon hiccupped.

"Shit, son. I thought you'd passed out."

Waylon started to cry, again—a drunk, stupid, kind of cry.

Clive grimaced.

Red did, too.

Loretta put her arm around the clown again, and he sobbed into her shirt. "Dammit, Clive," she whispered. "You know when he winds up how hard it is to get him to stop."

Which wasn't a lie.

The kid cried through Johnny, through George, and then Merle before he laid his head on the bar again.

"Go on," Clive urged Loretta. "Take care of your customers. I'll take care of sugar britches, here."

"Save the tough love for later. Okay? He's too drunk to remember it, anyway."

"And Jimmy?" Clive asked.

Loretta looked toward the office. "If Daddy were alive, he'd be ashamed of him."

"Want me to talk to him?"

Loretta shook her head. "I'll take care of my brother."

When Loretta was back behind the bar, she put a glass of water in front of Waylon, but the effort was useless. The kid was passed out, his drool puddling on the bar.

Red found an empty barstool next to Clive, took a seat, and put the Berretta on the bar. "Gun wasn't loaded."

"Never is." Clive went back to his tumbler, now filled with whiskey. A fresh bottle of Shiner Bock sat in front of Red, too. He watched Loretta, back at the tap, pouring beer.

She met his eyes. Thank you, she mouthed.

Red's mind went back to why he was here.

His stomach twisted.

"You, all right?" Clive asked.

Red shifted in his seat, the question catching him by surprise. It wasn't casual, not some effort to make small talk. The way Clive looked at him—the concern in his eyes—it was genuine. And it made him feel even worse.

Red glanced at the door. He should leave. He had what he needed. He'd put eyes on Loretta, got a sense of the place—the small staff, the lack of security—even the shotgun in Red's world wasn't much of a threat. He just needed the green light from Maddox to proceed, and he didn't need to wait here for it.

He ignored Clive, pushed back from his seat, threw some money on the bar.

But before he could put his billfold away, a man with a handlebar mustache approached him. He had a cowboy hat in hand, filled with cash—a few twenties, singles mostly.

"Wanted to catch you before you left," the man explained. "We're collecting money for Logan. His kid is in the hospital. I know you're not from these parts but thought you might want to help a fellow cowboy."

Red stared at the hat—the wadded-up bills. And suddenly, he understood why he felt connected to this place, these people.

It had nothing to do with the building or the music or the booze.

The place reminded him of his childhood, the community where he grew up—where people looked out for one another. Before his parents died, and he was forced to move away and make it on his own. A time in his life when people were good, kind. How he was none of those things. And how he hated himself for it.

He turned his back on the man and walked out the door.

Outside, the air was cold, typical for January. Red took off his Stetson, raked a hand through his hair while he stared up at the glass-paneled high rises that surrounded The Rose.

He could almost imagine what the honky-tonk had looked like years ago when Austin was still rural. When the squat, weathered building existed in an open field. When it was the focal point of the community, a place where ranch hands and locals came to socialize.

Before the funky boutiques, the high-end restaurants, the art galleries.

Before Maddox got here.

This is just another job, he tried to remind himself. Tomorrow, he'd be on his way to the next town, the next task, the next paycheck.

But in his gut, he knew this wasn't true. Something was different. *He* was different, and he didn't know how to come to terms with it.

Red's phone buzzed. He flipped it open, glanced at the screen.

A summons from Maddox. He wanted to see Red, confirm his marching orders.

He sighed before he put his Stetson back on and continued through the parking lot. Past the beat-up Chevys, the shiny

Harleys, and the semi-tractors from out-of-town truckers.

Until the gravel turned to dirt and the dirt opened into a construction site.

Bulldozers, mixers, cranes were littered around nearly completed high rises. Smells of drywall, fresh paint, and pro-pane from heaters filled the air. Elegant signs promised luxury condos and retail stores coming soon—the leasing options starting within the week.

When Red reached the office trailer, he climbed the steps, his boots clanging against the metal risers. He found Maddox inside, heels propped on a desk. His snakeskin boots looked lacquered underneath the fluorescent lights.

"When are you going to buy yourself some bull hides?" Red asked.

"The day you get a real phone."

"Old ways don't mean they're bad ways."

Red had always liked their banter, the way they started their meetings—casual, familiar. There was a comfortable rhythm to how they did things, too. Hell, he'd known the man for twenty years. Maybe he could reason with him, explain the merits of The Rose, why it was important for Maddox to come up with a plan to somehow leverage it.

"Change is good," Maddox continued. "Look what we've done for Austin—for the state of Texas."

The "we" part was true. He'd been doing Maddox's dirty work across the state—poisoning cattle, ruining crops, blackmail-ing people, killing if needed—anything to smooth the way for Maddox's endless string of real estate transactions. Red never had a problem with the jobs or the money from Maddox and his West Coast friends.

Until now.

"Locals won't look too kindly on those boots," Red said. "They don't do business with people they can't trust. Speaking of locals—"

"The locals." Maddox rolled his eyes. "Aging cowboys can't

afford these condos. Urban professionals, tech company executives, creatives—these are the kind of people I want to attract, which isn't going to happen with that honky-tonk relic sitting just beyond their windows."

Maddox dropped his feet to the floor. "I want to show you something." He walked over to a model that sat on top of a conference table. "This will be the crown jewel of the real estate development once we level The Rose."

Red joined him at the table, hoping to find a way to start the conversation again. But when he saw the model, he knew it was pointless.

Western World was three-dimensional. The exterior mirrored the rest of the tall high-rises. The interior had more than thirty bar stations, rows and rows of pool tables, ax-throwing lanes, a restaurant, and a mechanical bull-riding arena.

"Western World?" Red commented on the name. "The way you were going on about them urbanites, I thought you were trying to take the Tex out of Texas."

"People move out here for a western vibe. And we will give it to them—our version of it, anyway. Southwestern décor, fusion restaurants with just enough entertainment that it feels authentic. A place our condo residents can frequent after a long day at the office." Maddox grinned. "What do you think?"

It felt touristy, impersonal. No different than the other places Maddox had built. Red folded his arms and tried to tell Maddox just that, but he cut Red off again.

"I want you to burn it."

Red frowned. "Burn what?"

"The Rose. I want you to scorch it."

Maddox's "creative" methods, his ideas on how Red should execute his job, usually never bothered him. But this bothered Red. He sucked in a breath.

Maddox's face hardened. "Do you have a problem with that?"

The way Maddox looked at him told Red that twenty years working for the man meant nothing. They were friendly, but they weren't friends.

"Just surprised," Red said, trying his best to keep his tone neutral. "I thought the original plan was to lean on Loretta. Try to get her to sell the place."

"Been leaning on that woman for six months. I've seen the front end of her shotgun more than once. She'd just as soon die as give up the place her daddy built."

Red's mind went back to the bar—the pictures under the yellowing urethane. Generations had come to The Rose. When it was gone who would take care of Waylon when he was stupid again? Who would pass the hat for Logan's kid? And then there were the old-timers, like Clive. Maddox wasn't just destroying a building, he was destroying a community, a way of life. And he was using Red to do it.

"Give me a chance to talk to her," Red said, trying to buy some time. "Get her to *our* way of thinking."

Maddox shook his head. "I'm on a deadline. Condo, retail models open this weekend. Lease prices can be higher with my plan in place. Time for talking is over."

Red glanced at the door. He could walk away. He had some money set aside. No one stayed in this business forever. But the minute he considered it, he knew that wasn't true.

No one walked away from Maddox.

A fixer with a conscience was an occupational hazard Maddox couldn't afford. He would consider Red a liability. Maddox would hire someone else to finish the job after he finished Red.

Out of options, Red simply echoed Maddox's request. "Burn it."

Maddox's focus returned to the 3D model. He adjusted one of the pieces.

Red turned to leave.

"And Red," Maddox looked up at him. "Make sure Loretta's inside the place when you do it."

* * *

Red made his way back to the bar, his eyes fixed on the neon sign. It flickered, fighting to remain illuminated. When he reached the gravel parking lot, it was nearly empty, except for Clive, who was struggling to get Waylon into a rusted-out pickup truck.

Red rushed over to help him.

"Damn back ain't what it used to be," Clive mumbled.

Waylon wasn't doing Clive any favors. He was dead weight, his arms and legs flopping around like a rag doll.

When the clown was settled, Clive heaved the passenger door closed. The hinges squeaked in protest.

"Where the hell did you come from, anyway?" Clive glanced toward Maddox's construction site and seemed to try to make sense of it. "Thought you left hours ago."

"Came back for another drink," Red lied. He looked at his truck still in the parking lot. The windows had started to ice over.

"Place closed?" Red asked, quickly.

"Loretta's cleaning up. Bet she'd still pour you one, if you went inside."

Red scanned the parking lot. Three vehicles, two—once Clive pulled away. Red's truck and Old Bluesides. Guess Loretta wasn't lying to Waylon about driving her brother's truck to work. "Jimmy there, too?"

Clive shook his head. "Evelyn picked him up about an hour ago."

"You don't say."

"Girl is bold, I'll give her that."

Red looked at Waylon through the window. "Poor bastard."

"By God's grace, he was still passed out when it happened."

Clive pulled out a pack of Marlboros, offered a cigarette to Red, who accepted. Then, he handed Red his lighter.

It was plastic. Nothing fancy. Red flicked the wheel, watched the flame—the tapering shape, the blue and red and orange hues—a reminder of Maddox's awful task. The idea still bothered him deep in his gut. He sighed before he put the cigarette between his lips, lit the tip, and inhaled.

"Think he'll be all right?" Red asked, his eyes on Waylon.

"Guess it depends on what you mean by all right. Kid gets squirrely with a pistol every time he catches Evelyn catting around. It's always with someone from the bar. Way I figure it, life for him won't get better until he gets rid of her."

"About that—" Red flicked his cigarette, the ash disappearing into the darkness. "If Loretta knows the pistol ain't loaded, why the shotgun?"

Clive sighed. "It's simple, really. Evelyn catting around makes the kid feel small enough already. Imagine if Loretta didn't take him seriously, too?"

Red figured it made about as much sense as anything else he'd heard this evening.

"What about you?" Clive asked, cigarette bobbing between his lips.

"My Python's loaded," Red said.

"I'm not talking about your piece." Clive paused, seemed to study Red. "Just looks like you're grappling with something. That's all."

Red took a long drag from his cigarette, focused on the taste—cherry, wood, the hint of barley—while he considered the best way to answer Clive. "Guess man reaches a certain age when he takes stock of his life."

"And you're not happy with the inventory?"

Red shrugged.

"Yeah." Clive nodded more to himself than Red. "Felt that way when I came back from Nam. Lost my squad in Khe Sanh. Walked around with a lot of guilt, a lot of regret." Clive cleared his throat. "Want some advice from an old man?"

"Sure," Red said.

"Regret is bullshit. It's a useless emotion. And it doesn't change the past."

"And redemption?"

Clive shrugged. "Guess it's up to you to decide what that looks like."

Waylon shifted against the seat.

"Better get him home," Clive said. "Before he winds up again." He climbed into the pickup truck and cranked down the window. "Much obliged for the help, friend."

Friend—the word cut Red like a knife.

As the pickup rattled away, Red looked down at Clive's lighter, still in his hand, and walked toward The Rose.

A week later, Red returned to The Rose. It took the fire department that long to clean up the debris and open the parking lot.

That night, he'd gone back inside the bar, had that drink with Loretta. She'd told him about her daddy, how he'd been a Vietnam veteran like Clive. How Clive had looked out for her and Jimmy after he'd passed. And the responsibility she felt to the people who still came to her daddy's establishment, a place named after her late mother.

Truth was, it didn't take much soul searching after that. Hell, he reckoned he'd made the decision on the walk back from Maddox's construction site.

He couldn't burn the place. He felt a kinship to these people— to Clive, to Loretta, even to the clown—something he hadn't felt since he was a kid.

"Did ya hear?" Clive eyed Red over his tumbler of whiskey.

"Hear what?" Red asked.

"Papers said it was one of them kerosene heaters that started that-there fire. Took out them fancy buildings. Trailer with Mr. Maddox, too. Damn miracle The Rose is still standing."

"A miracle," Red agreed. His mind went to Clive's plastic lighter still in his pocket.

The guy with the handlebar mustache took a seat next to Red.

"Hey, Loretta—" Red pointed to the man and Clive. "Next round is on me."

She smiled. "You got it."

"Thanks, friend," Clive said.

"The name is Red."

"Much obliged, Red." Clive pointed to the man with the handlebar mustache. "That-there is Charlie."

Charlie and Red exchanged nods.

"Did you hear about Logan's kid?" Charlie asked. "Someone paid his medical bills."

Red arched a brow. "You don't say."

Regret was bullshit—Red agreed with Clive—and he certainly couldn't undo the past, undo the things he'd done. But he had to admit, it felt good to take Maddox's blood money and do something decent with it.

Loretta brought their drinks—beer for Red, whiskey for Clive, tequila for Charlie.

Charlie raised his glass. "A toast to miracles."

"Two in one week," Clive said.

Three—if you counted Red.

Red still didn't know if there was redemption for scoundrels like him or if he even deserved it. But he figured if he mirrored the kindness he'd seen as a kid, the kindness he'd seen at The Rose—maybe he'd be all right.

"Where's Jimmy?" A boozy voice yelled.

Red looked over at Clive, who didn't bother to look up from his whiskey. He just sighed and shook his head. "Here we go, again."

ABOUT THE EDITORS

MICHAEL BRACKEN has edited several previous crime fiction anthologies, including the Anthony Award-nominated *The Eyes of Texas: Private Eyes from the Panhandle to the Piney Woods* and the three-volume *Fedora* series. Additionally, he is the author of eleven books and more than thirteen hundred short stories, including crime fiction published in *Alfred Hitchcock's Mystery Magazine, Black Cat Mystery Magazine, Ellery Queen's Mystery Magazine,* and *The Best American Mystery Stories.* He has two-stepped in dance halls and honky-tonks throughout central Texas.

GARY PHILLIPS has published various novels, comics, short stories, worked in television, and edited or co-edited several anthologies, including the Anthony-winning *The Obama Inheritance: Fifteen Stories of Conspiracy Noir. Violent Spring,* his debut effort some twenty-seven years ago, was named one of the essential crime novels of Los Angeles. His latest book is the retro pulpy goodness *Matthew Henson and the Ice Temple of Harlem.* He's been sober and not so much in a few juke joints in Clarksdale in the Mississippi Delta and one in Watts, California.

ABOUT THE CONTRIBUTORS

While **TREY R. BARKER** frequently taps his own history for his stories, this is his most autobiographical yet. From playing clubs and tonks in college to his mother urging him to sit behind some drums and play along at a club when he was in junior high, Trey has spent many a night in some version of just about every joint in this collection. He has argued musical turn-arounds with Buddy Guy in Chicago over sammiches, and argued with George Thorogood about the local blues scene in Corpus Christi over middling whiskey. He wrote parts of his first published novel in a joint in Denver and met Ray Wylie Hubbard at a joint in LaSalle, Illinois.

For forty-plus years **JONATHAN BROWN** has played drums in juke joints, honky-tonks, bars, house parties, hen houses and once even sang (drunk) in an outhouse. In 2019 Jonathan released *The Big Crescendo—A Lou Crasher Mystery* (Down & Out Books) and in 2020 released *Don't Shoot the Drummer* (Down & Out Books). Currently, Jonathan is knee-deep penning the next Crasher book. Working title: *Drums, Guns N Money.*

S.A. COSBY is an award-winning author from southeastern Virginia. His work has appeared in numerous anthologies and magazines, including *Thuglit, Ellery Queen's Mystery Magazine, Lockdown,* and *The Faking of the President.* He is the author of *My Darkest Prayer* and *Blacktop Wasteland.*

JOHN M. FLOYD's short stories have appeared in *Alfred Hitchcock's Mystery Magazine, Ellery Queen's Mystery Magazine, The Strand Magazine, The Saturday Evening Post*, three editions of *The Best American Mystery Stories*, and many other publications. He is also an Edgar nominee, a four-time Derringer Award winner, a three-time Pushcart Prize nominee, the 2018 recipient of the Edward D. Hoch Memorial Golden Derringer Award for lifetime achievement, and the author of nine books. John grew up just down the road from some of the jukiest tonks in Mississippi. Visit him at JohnMFloyd.com.

Judge **DEBRA H. GOLDSTEIN** authors Kensington's Sarah Blair mystery series, including recently published *Three Treats Too Many*; 2020 Silver Falchion finalist *Two Bites Too Many*; and January 2019 *Woman's World* Book of the Week, *One Taste Too Many*. Debra also wrote *Should Have Played Poker* and 2012 IPPY Award-winning *Maze in Blue*. Her short stories have been chosen as Agatha, Anthony, and Derringer finalists. When Debra moved to Alabama, she discovered its civil rights history, the college football rivalry between Alabama and Auburn, and Gip's Place, Alabama's last original juke joint. Founded in 1952 by Henry "Gip" Gipson, Gip's Place was a Saturday night haven of music and fellowship, despite what was going on in the world, until Gip's death in 2019. Find out more about Debra at DebraHGoldstein.com.

GAR ANTHONY HAYWOOD is the Shamus and Anthony award-winning author of thirteen crime novels, including the Aaron Gunner private-eye series and Joe and Dottie Loudermilk mysteries. His short fiction has been included in *The Best American Mystery Stories* anthologies, and Booklist has called him "a writer who has always belonged in the upper echelon of American crime fiction." Haywood's seventh Aaron Gunner mystery, *Good Man Gone Bad*, was published by Prospect Park in Fall 2019.

PENNY MICKELBURY is the author of thirteen published novels and a collection of short stories, and she has contributed stories and articles to a variety of magazines and collections. Two of her novels are historical fiction, though most of them are mysteries, one of which, *Death's Echoes*, the fifth book in the Mimi Patterson/Gianna Maglione Mystery Series, won the 2019 IPPY Bronze Medal in the national Mystery/Thriller category. The sixth book in the series, *Can't Die But Once*, was released in December 2020 and is a finalist for the Georgia Writer of the Year Award in the mystery/suspense category. Penny had her first, last, and only taste of moonshine at a juke joint in Athens, Georgia, while attending college at the University of Georgia. Shooting erupted during her last visit to the juke, and she slipped away before police arrived. The Atlanta native lives in Los Angeles.

WILLIAM DYLAN POWELL (texasmischief.com) is a former Lubbock bartender who writes dark, and sometimes funny, stories set in Texas. A Houston resident today, his work has appeared in a variety of unsavory publications. His grandfather once had a little band that played Hank Williams songs outside of San Augustine, Texas, on Saturday nights. The pastor demanded he stop the shows because Sunday service attendance was hurting. You don't say no to the pastor.

KIMBERLY B. RICHARDSON is the author of *Tales from a Goth Librarian I and II*; *The Decembrists*; *Mabon/Pomegranate*; *Jackie Verona: A Murder of Gypsies*; *Open A; Chinese Food and Gypsy Jazz; Dark Passions; Order of the Black Silk Trilogy*; and *The Path of a Tea Traveler*. She also has stories in multiple anthologies. Kimberly was the 2015 David McCrosky Volunteer Photographer in Residence for Elmwood Cemetery in Memphis, Tennessee. Kimberly is the founder and owner of Viridian Tea Company and a World Tea Academy Certified Tea Specialist. She currently resides in Colorado.

STACY WOODSON made her crime fiction debut in *Ellery Queen Mystery Magazine*'s Department of First Stories and won the 2018 Readers Award. Since her debut, she has placed stories in *Mickey Finn, Mystery Weekly, Woman's World*, and *EQMM* among other anthologies and publications. When she was stationed in South Korea, Stacy spent time at a tonk called the Grand Ole Opry in Itaewon. It was an old GI hangout that had been around for nearly fifty years, and she always loved that they played "The Star Spangled Banner" at midnight. You can visit Stacy at StacyWoodson.com.

On the following pages are a few
more great titles from the
Down & Out Books publishing family.

For a complete list of books and to
sign up for our newsletter,
go to DownAndOutBooks.com.

The Great Filling Station Holdup
Crime Fiction Inspired by the Songs of Jimmy Buffett
Josh Pachter, Editor

Down & Out Books
February 2021
978-1-64396-181-1

Editor Josh Pachter presents sixteen short crime stories by six-teen popular and up-and-coming crime writers, each story based on a song from one of the twenty-nine studio albums Jimmy has released over the last half century.

Including stories by Leigh Lundin, Josh Pachter, Rick Ollerman, Michael Bracken, Don Bruns, Alison McMahan, Bruce Robert Coffin, Lissa Marie Redmond, Elaine Viets, Robert J. Randisi, Laura Oles, Isabella Maldonado, Jeffery Hess, Neil Plakcy, John M. Floyd, and M.E. Browning.

Moonlight Rises
A Dick Moonlight PI Thriller
Vincent Zandri

Down & Out Books
March 2021
978-1-64396-189-7

Dick Moonlight is dead for real this time. Thanks to a trio of masked thugs in a dark downtown Albany alley, he's purchased a one-way ticket to the Pearly Gates—that is, until he feels his floating spirit painfully pulled back into his bruised but breathing body. And that's when the real trouble starts.

The Cold War is heating up once again in Vincent Zandri's latest thriller. *Moonlight Rises* is a fast-paced, whip-smart tale of a guy who can't always remember getting into trouble—and can't seem to stay out of it. An unputdownable mystery that's sure to keep you up all night…in a good way.

Trigger Switch
Bryon Quertermous

All Due Respect, an imprint of
Down & Out Books
March 2021
978-1-64396-190-3

Dominick Prince has been a magnet for trouble his entire life. A series of poor life choices and their violent consequences have crushed his spirit. Desperate to outrun this burgeoning rage before it fully consumes him, Dominick accepts an offer he doesn't trust from an old high school classmate.

Dutchy Kent says he wants to make one last-ditch effort to prove his acting chops by mounting the New York City debut of a play based on one of Dominick's stories, but the true story involves the real estate empire of a notorious Queens drug dealer and $1.2 million in cash.

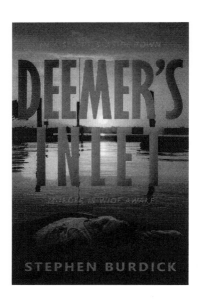

Deemer's Inlet
Stephen Burdick

Shotgun Honey, an imprint of
Down & Out Books
August 2020
978-1-64396-104-0

Far from the tourist meccas of Ft. Lauderdale and Miami Beach, a chief of police position in the quiet, picturesque town of Deemer's Inlet on the Gulf coast of Florida seemed ideal for Eldon Quick—until the first murder.

The crime and a subsequent killing force Quick to call upon his years of experience as a former homicide detective in Miami. Soon after, two more people are murdered and Quick believes a serial killer is on the loose. As Quick works to uncover the identity and motive of the killer, he must contend with an understaffed police force, small town politics, and curious residents.